SEARCHING FOR ANNA

By Michaele Benedict

ISBN **978-1-4357-1017-7**

For DrDoogie, SherlockJr, AnnasUnc and
WebSleuths, and especially for
all the families who never got to see
a certain child grow up.

TABLE OF CONTENTS

Searching for Anna

By Michaele Benedict

Prologue, Chapter 20 and design by Douglas M. French

Anna Christian Waters, an effervescent five-year-old, was the daughter of a young San Francisco physician and his writer wife. She was just beginning her fifth month of kindergarten when she disappeared from home Jan. 16, 1973. No sign of her was ever found, but the National Center for Missing and Exploited Children and the San Mateo County Sheriff's Department lists the case as a probable non-family abduction.

the creek all the way to the ocean, but say they don't see how they could have missed anything. Sgt. Maguire asks about the father.

Fishermen search the creek, find a rooster corpse and a sock, but it's not Anna's sock. Mother and stepfather drive the school bus route to see where the farm could be watched surreptitiously. Neighbors search the creek around the tree house.

Appendix – Page 219: Links and references. Acknowledgements. A list of people in the story and where they are now. Maps, Purisima Creek Road. Anna's drawings.

Links and References

Web page: www.searchingforanna.com

National Center for Missing and Exploited Children
Gerald Nance, case worker
GNANCE@ncmec.org
Case No. NCMC601935
1-800-8435678

WebSleuths Spotlight Cases
www.websleuths.com/forums/forumdisplay.php?f+104

Detective James Gilletti, San Mateo County Missing
Persons Unit
(650) 313-4911
Case 73-0484
JGILLETTI@co.sanmateo.ca.us

National Crime Information Center, FBI
Case Number 205458221

Facebook (Nancy's page):
www.facebook.com/group.php?gid=6080498620

United Nations Convention on the Rights of the Child:
www.rehydrate.org/facts/convention_full.htm

Vanished Children's Alliance 1-800-8435678
www.vca.org

Half Moon Bay Review article, 2006
http://hmbreview.com/articles/2006/09/20/news/local_news/story02.txt

MySpace (15 million daily log-ins, 10,593 page views
per second)
    Maureen's page: www.myspace.com/reuniteanna
    Gina's page: www.myspace.com/annachristianwaters

YouTube Videos (three) by Gina_M:
        http://www.youtube.com/watch?v=x6mAPR5Pspg

Attempt the end, and never stand to doubt;
Nothing's so hard but search will find it out.
"Seek and Find", Robert Herrick (1591-1674)

"Don't be sad. Be happy, like me."
Anna Christian Waters

Prologue

By Doug French

The story of Searching for Anna, when viewed from a literary standpoint, may be a flawed work. It suffers from the limitations that the truth always does: It does not follow simple outlines and character development. The story does not "flow". And most importantly, you know how the story ends (in this manuscript, at least) – we are still searching for Anna as of this writing.

What this manuscript does do is provide a brutally honest telling of how one family has searched for their missing daughter. It exposes the joys and the pains, the progress and the missteps, the hopes and the heartbreaks. There are heroes and villains. There are sorrows and reasons to rejoice.

Most importantly, it shows how one family can suffer the tragedy of a daughter's disappearance and still refuse to bear the title of Victim (with a capital V). Victims are helpless and at the mercy of others. When the search for Anna became "old news" to law enforcement and society as a whole, the family took matters into their own hands and continued the hunt themselves. For that, they are my heroes.

I met Anna's family one year after her disappearance. I was sympathetic to the family's plight, but I was a teenager with nothing to offer but sympathy. Decades later, I was reminded of Anna's disappearance when I saw a television show concerning an unidentified woman who was known as "Sharon Marshall" who had been kidnapped, molested, raised as a daughter and ultimately killed by a monster of a man named Franklin Delano Floyd. The details of "Sharon" made me wonder if Sharon and Anna might be the same person. I delicately contacted Anna's mother and questioned her about details that may have linked the two cases – as delicately as one can when someone is ultimately asking if she thought that her daughter may have suffered the horrific fate that befell Sharon. Further research has shown that Anna and Sharon are two different people. However, that research also opened up new possibilities in the search for Anna that had not been explored. Furthermore, that research has convinced me that an answer to the question "What happened to Anna?" can still be uncovered three decades after her disappearance.

This manuscript is written to document what has occurred over those last three decades. It has been written to help other families who may find themselves in similar circumstances and need the reassurance that they are not alone during their tribulation. It is written to show a human interest story behind the all-too-frequent headlines involving missing children. It is a celebration of the great strides that we as a society have made in providing a safe environment for children in the years since Anna disappeared and an indication of the progress that has yet to be made.

But ultimately, this is a book written with an target audience of one: A forty-year- old woman with brown hair and brown eyes and distant memories of a loving family, a farmhouse on a creek, and a not-so-bright dog named Saturn…

CHAPTER ONE

On January 16, 1973, my daughter, Anna Christian Waters, disappeared from our home in Purisima Canyon, a rural area south of Half Moon Bay, California. The search for Anna has continued ever since that time. No trace of her has ever been found, though we found many other things while looking. This is the story of our search.

Anna Christian Waters was born at 4:44 P.M. September 25, 1967, at the University of California Hospital in San Francisco. We pronounced her name with a broad A, as in "swan". She was the first and only child of George Waters, who was completing a medical internship at San Francisco General Hospital. Anna's birth made me a grand multipara, a mother of many, or so it said on the door of the hospital room. Waiting at home were Anna's brothers, Nonda, nine years old, and Eddie, six, who had been born in Greece in the five years I lived in Athens and Thessaloniki.

Although he had lovingly prepared for Anna's birth, building and polishing a redwood cradle with a sunburst woodburned on the headboard, George left home shortly after Anna's first birthday, deeply troubled, and never returned. He lived in a hotel room in San Francisco's seedy Tenderloin District (roughly bordered by Geary, Polk, Taylor and Market streets) with an elderly gentleman he considered his mentor.

When George had been gone several months, Joseph Ford, a visiting friend of a friend, came down Winfield Street on an errand, saw me with the three children (probably throwing my hands in the air) and surmised that I could do with some help. He moved into the small yellow house at 83 Winfield, a move which signified either great trust or great desperation on both our parts. He went to Oregon to collect his belongings and returned to San Francisco to step comfortably into the role of paterfamilias at the age of twenty-seven.

Joe would zip one-year-old Anna into his jacket and putter through the Mission District on his small motorcycle, at times reaching an astonishing 25 miles per hour. In November of 1968, Joe had Anna in his jacket, both boys on back of the bike, and bags of groceries wherever they would fit, with a turkey balanced on the handlebars. The trip down Bernal Hill to the grocery store with the three children was easy enough, but trying to get back up the hill was a different matter. A policeman stopped Joe as he was pushing the comically-laden motorcycle up Elsie Street, but then just stood there with pad and pen in his hand, looking at the children and the turkey and shaking his head at Joe. Finally, the policeman said "You KNOW you can't do this. You KNOW you can't do this."

It seems reckless now, when infants aren't allowed to leave the hospital without proper car seats, when you can't ride a bicycle without a helmet. But we never left the children alone day or night; they were our best friends and constant companions. We wanted them to have courage and daring and fun, and we didn't want to make them afraid.

In 1971, we were not happy with the fact that the boys were going to be bussed away from their neighborhood school. We decided to teach the boys ourselves. We found a correspondence school for elementary grades, the Calvert School, which operated out of Baltimore and which provided everything from textbooks to rulers. We bought a 35-foot school bus at auction and converted it into a camper, complete with a 77-key piano, since Eddie was taking piano lessons at the San Francisco Conservatory of Music.

In the bus log, Anna wrote the first of her "Lo" letters--pages full of LOLOLO which perplexed and delighted us. Sometimes she would ask us to mail them to her particular friends. Gloria Barron wrote back "I LOLOLOLO LOVE you", and perhaps that was just what the letters meant. The LO letters could have been anything from binary code to, well, nothing at all, but the family called them Lo letters, as in "Lo and behold!" The letters continued until Anna went to kindergarten and learned to spell her name.

We went to visit friends and relatives all over the two coasts and the southern part of the United States. We went up to Oregon, down to Los Angeles, across the desert to Tennessee, through the Great Smoky Mountains, up to Philadelphia and Baltimore, back to Tennessee, and finally westward to Half Moon Bay, California, where our friends Phil and Elizabeth were going to let us have their house on a beautiful ranch in Purisima Canyon.

In September, 1972, Anna started kindergarten at Hatch School in Half Moon Bay. Nonda and Ed informed us that there was more to school than books and lessons, (namely, friends, the school band and football) so they went back to school, too, Ed to Cunha Intermediate School and Nonda to Half Moon Bay High School. We parked the bus outside the house and bought a van from a junkyard in San Francisco. Joe and the boys repaired the van on the street in San Francisco, covered up the rust with cans of spray paint, and drove home to Purisima Canyon. Resurrected junk, the registration called the van.

I signed up as a kindergarten aide at Hatch School, and Joe, ever resourceful, started following lumber trucks, looking for carpentry jobs.

On September 16th, 1972, Joe and I were married in a tree house he and the boys built over Purisima Creek. Our friends George and Poki came down to officiate at the homegrown service, and we all sang "Home on the Range", since that was the only song to which everyone knew the words.

Purisima Canyon was an idyllic setting. Fog would wash down the hillside as if painted on by a white-soaked brush, changing the trees to gray-green shapes with silvery trunks. This pastel foliage would change with the wind minute by minute until the sun cut through the moving scrim.

The women of the three houses, Peggy, Suzanne and I, wore long skirts to garden and do our chores. We sewed, canned, raised chickens and lived a life which in some ways might have belonged to our grandmothers.

The three men, John the fisherman, Suzanne's Bill and my Joe, were in charge of carpentry, firewood, and the spring, which sometimes became clogged with leaves, cutting off the household water supply. The men took care of the compost piles, and they were responsible for holding down jobs and for dealing with the motorcycle club, the horse people, and the hunters who used various buildings and trails on the farm.

The children, Peggy's two older girls, Shawn and Gina, and Nonda and Eddie and Anna, went to school seven miles north, in Half Moon Bay. The big yellow school bus which looked so much like our own bus, sitting idle in the driveway and waiting to be sold, took the children up on the ridge, over the winding, narrow Higgins Canyon Road and from there into town.

(Family 9/17/72: (from left to right) Michaele, Anna, Joe, Nonda, Eddie)

Nonda, though too young to get a learner's driving permit, was allowed to drive on Purisima Creek Road, though the fence was never the same after he backed into it. And since he could not legally drive out in the real world and sometimes needed transportation from after-school activities when Joe was at work, I once again tried to learn to drive, shaking, trembling, crying and praying but finally passing my driver's test by one point. I gave the Motor Vehicles examiner a Wells Fargo badge the bank had given me and all its clients at its inaugural in Half Moon Bay.

In October 1972, our family and other members of a food-purchasing collective, Farmers' Feed Hams, put on a melodrama, "The Saga of Spanishtown Sue", in which Anna portrayed a daisy growing in a garden. The production was notable for several reasons. The play epitomized our innocent, cheerful life in Purisima Canyon. Under the guise of comedy, it dealt with a number of opinions regarding landlords, religion and morality. The primary theme, however, was child abduction, a subject we never thought to deal with in real life.

January 16, 1973, changed all our lives forever. Except for the wrenching emotions we all experienced and still, to some degree, experience after all these years, the story of the long search for Anna might be some kind of mystery novel, complete with private detectives, crazy people, psychics, and the waxing and waning of our hopes after decades of futile efforts to shed light on the puzzle.

Many of these futile efforts remained private. After a while, it was difficult to talk about it. An odd kind of emotional isolation gripped the family, and eventually the family members parted and made separate lives for themselves.

"How can you stand it, not knowing?" people would sometimes ask. And then they would fall silent, because they couldn't stand it themselves.

CHAPTER TWO

Half Moon Bay, California, is the center of a group of coastal communities located only a 45-minute drive south from San Francisco. Access over a winding and sometimes crumbling section of the Coast Highway known as Devil's Slide keeps it from being an easy jaunt from San Francisco and points north. Though the community and its Pumpkin Festival, Pentecost Celebration and flower markets attract many tourists, the heart of the Coastside in 1973 was still rural. On the back roads, Coastsiders still drove slowly in order not to spook the horses.

The highway runs over what was the Ocean Shore Railroad right of way until the time of the Great Quake of 1906, though the railroad folded because of financial problems, not earthquake problems. Near the two saddle cuts blasted into the rocky foothills of the Coastal range, the road narrows and the cliffs drop down perilously to the Pacific Ocean. A tunnel through the mountain is expected to be completed in 2010.

Just south of Devil's Slide is Montara, the northernmost of the Coastside Communities, and then Moss Beach, which has a few stores and a tiny airport, then El Granada, which is called Princeton west of the highway and which has Pillar Point Harbor. Half Moon Bay is next. In 1973, Half Moon Bay had a handful of churches, two grocery stores, several little shops on Main Street, but no fast food places, no motels or bed and breakfast places, no tourist attractions. There were nurseries and fields of flowers, pumpkins, Brussels sprouts and artichokes.

Continuing south, the Pacific Ocean shimmers its way to the horizon. On the left of the highway are three canyons, Higgins, Purisima, and Tunitas, and then the farming communities of San Gregorio and Pescadero and, inland, La Honda. The next coastal town south is Davenport, 40 miles away, and then Santa Cruz.

Between Half Moon Bay and Santa Cruz, there are three roads leading across the coastal range to the east: Highway 92, as winding and narrow as Devil's Slide, but without the rocks which bounce onto the road; A convoluted, tree-shaded road up Tunitas Creek Road to Skyline on the ridge, and then Highway 84 from San Gregorio.

Purisima Creek Road runs perpendicular to the Coast Highway about 40 miles south of San Francisco. The road meanders some 30 feet above Purisima Creek. The name dates from the time of the

Spanish land grants when the area was called Canada de Verde y Arroyo de la Purisima.

The creek, fed by springs from the ridge above it, passes under Purisima Creek Road just before the road itself doubles back, rises up the coastal range to the north and becomes Higgins Canyon Road, which winds back to Half Moon Bay.

Half Moon Bay, once known as Spanishtown, still has a large Hispanic community, as well as many Portuguese from the Azores, so many, in fact, that there is an all-Portuguese television channel on the local cable service. Portuguese and Spanish names abound: Alves, Avila, Azevido, Bettencourt, Cardoza, Cunha, Machado, Nunez, Souza.

The banks of Purisima Creek are a herbalist's delight. Besides the ever-present red alder, water birch and blackberry, there is figwort, and redwood sorrel. Sword fern and bracken fern grow next to the water, and there are patches of bergamot mint, watercress and miner's lettuce. The delicate blue of wild forget-me-not is everywhere, as is horsetail fern, which can grow even through asphalt and will cut your hands if you try to pull it.

Periwinkle, violets, trillium, and an occasional wild California rose add notes of color to the deep, moist green which persists near the creek even when the hills have turned brown in the rainless California summer.

Fishermen fish for trout in the creek, which runs shallow most of the year, passing through a number of fences and log dams, underneath Verde Road and Highway One and on to the Pacific Ocean. For a while, a bachelor flock of mallards could be heard up and down the creek, their quacking like raucous laughter. And, rarely, a seagull, pelican, crane or other exotic bird is lured inland by the cool water and lush growth.

In the fields nearby, one sees horses and cows and many blackfaced sheep, some of them projects for the county fair and Future Farmers of America. Most of the farms have at least a few chickens: White leghorns, barred rocks, the sturdy Rhode Island Red, or exotic silkies and Araucanas with their colored eggs.

Where one of our neighbors used to live, there is now a model ranch, Elkus Ranch, at which local school children learn about animals and farming.

Up on the ridge there used to be an oil well and pump, but no one seemed to know whether it worked or not, and no one knew who it belonged to or how long it had been there.

The fog from the ocean usually dissipates before it gets very far up Purisima Creek Road, but once in a while it flows down from the ridge like a cottony white tidal wave, making the gold or green of the meadows into a canvas of pastels.

Purisima was once a town with a school, a mill and a post office, but now all that remains of the town is an overgrown graveyard where Purisima Creek Road and Verde Road cross.

At the end of the road, just before the woods, where the road doubles back, is the farm where we lived. From Purisima Creek Road you can look down on the houses and barns. Running right up to the road is a meadow, neatly fenced, and the big hay barn, white, capably restored. The farm road continues past a building which was once a water mill, and then over the bridge and past the horse barn.

The road continues up the hill, mostly hidden by manzanita brush, broom and eucalyptus trees, to what once was a hunters' cabin. On the other side of the truck bridge over Purisima Creek are cottages which were ramshackle coops and pens when we lived there.

Continuing back from the creek toward the main road, there is a Queen Anne-style house. For a long time, there was a mountain of abalone shells next to this house (which we sometimes called the Big House), since John, who had lived there, dived for abalone in season and ran the Abalone Shop at Pillar Point Harbor. The malodorous hill of shells disappeared quickly after it was offered to the San Francisco public television station for their fund-raising auction one year.

Next to the Queen Anne was a cabin, repaired and remodeled after a resident, taking a shower, leaned against the bathroom wall and wound up in the living room. Next to the road is the one-bedroom house we lived in, fenced with grapestake, with a gazebo and a sheep pen in the yard. Old moss-covered apple and plum trees droop near the fence. An exuberant wild rose hedge once burgeoned between the house and the road.

Seen from the road, it could be a farm anywhere in the United States, Virginia, Massachusetts, Oregon, white, freshly painted, with dense greenery marking the path of the creek. When we lived there, the place consisted of the three houses in varying states of disrepair, the two barns, the millhouse with the millwheel falling apart but the building more or less intact, several half-fallen coops and an outhouse.

The yellow frame house where we lived was just down a small bank from Purisima Creek Road, where three mailboxes, Box 313, A, B, and C, stood. You walked directly from the gravel driveway into the living room of the house. In the winter, there would be a pile of rubber boots beside the front door, for slogging down the muddy paths of the farm.

The living room had an enormous window on the south side, looking out on the meadow and on the hill. There was a brick fireplace which drew pretty well most of the time, the only heat except for small electric heaters. There was a couch, a beanbag chair, and a television set which sometimes produced two or three blurry images, depending on how energetically someone outside turned the antenna. "No, back the other way! There! No, you passed it. Go the other way!"

The small piano we had bolted to the steel wall of our bus-camper stood at one end of the room, much the worse for wear. Eddie and I would play on this piano by the hour, sometimes joined by Nonda on the drums. More than once, Anna volunteered to be a cymbal stand for Nonda, holding up his solitary Ziltjian with a finger through the center hole (and sometimes a finger from the other hand in her ear.) Continuing toward the back of the house, away from the road, was a glassed-in porch where Joe and I slept. Bamboo shades covered the windows on two walls, and a cardboard wardrobe held our clothing, mostly jeans, sweaters, and long skirts. This room had a door giving onto the fenced back yard.

To the right of the living room was the kitchen, a dining room with a window seat looking out on the back yard, the bathroom, and a small hallway which led to a back porch. The path from the porch ran down the hill to Suzanne's and my garden, then to Peggy and John Koepf's house, the Queen Anne, and to Suzanne's house next door.

The large room off the hallway was the children's room. Nonda and Ed each had a twin bed and a closet on opposite sides of the room. On the side nearest the hallway was Anna's area. This included a bed Joe had built, a bed ascended by steps, with a cupboard underneath.

In January of 1973, the farm, still called the Pimentel Ranch and not yet named Rancho Canada Verde, was in transition. We had rented the house while the 150 acres was in probate, and we paid rent to Bank of America, which was administering the estate. The landlord, Lindsay Mickles, had recently bought the place for, gossip had it, three quarters of a million dollars. John, Peggy and their children, Shawn, Gina and Daisy, had moved from the Queen Anne which they rented and had bought a house in Montara, north of Half Moon Bay. Suzanne, who lived in the house next door, was coping alone with the wood stove and her worm farm.

The five of us, Nonda, 14 years old, Eddie, 11, Anna, 5, Joe and I were not sure how long we would be able to rent the house near the road. The new owner wanted to develop the ranch and was beginning, in subtle and not-so-subtle ways, to nudge us away.

CHAPTER THREE

On January 16, it rained in the morning, but Joe left at about seven for work. The children left for school at 7:30, and I fed the animals, noticing as I crossed the bridge to the chicken coop how high the creek was.

At about 10 A.M., I was working on a poem.

After a fearsome night of gales
And blowing rain and unexpected noises,
I girded up in waterproofs from head to toe
And went out to feed the animals.
The chickens had a sudden moat, iron-red and rushing,
Hiding the path, sweeping along
New growth, old woods,
Submerging thickets of hemlock and stinging nettles.
Everywhere, downhill ditches
Had appeared overnight, full of water,
And the friendly babble of the creek
Was an urgent thunder, wide and deep,
Carrying pilings, meadow, branches,
Almost up to the mill wheel
Which might any minute begin to--

I heard screams. I dropped the notebook, pulled on my boots, and ran down to the bridge. Sandy Quinn, who had come to feed her horse, had been attacked by old Hulk, the rooster. I had raised Hulk in a cardboard box containing mirrors, clocks, and other mother-substitutes, but he had grown into a belligerent adolescent and had been banished to the henhouse on the far side of Purisima Creek.

I brought Sandy back to the house. When Bruce Coggins, the blacksmith, came, Sandy gathered her courage and returned to the stables, but the rooster was unrelenting. The blacksmith grabbed the rooster by the head, wrung his neck, and tossed him into the creek.

Unsettled by all this, I turned back to the poem.

Screams from the creek! Cold terror
in the cries for help! Is someone
washing away? I run to see,
out in the rain with no coat:

"Hang on! I'm coming!"
And the old rooster is scaring Sandy.
That's all it is. Saturn, the dog, frightens
the rooster away....
Almost up to the mill wheel
--which might at any minute
Begin to turn, ghostly half-demented fragments
Whispering threats and promises out of another time.

At about 11 A.M., our old friends Arlene and Asya and their baby, Baris, came down from San Francisco for a visit. Joe returned around noon, unable to get a day's carpentry in because of the rain.

At about 12:20 we heard the school bus stop on the road above the house. We continued our conversation, listening for Anna's footsteps.

She came in the front door, wearing brown shoes with white knee socks, a green dress her paternal grandparents had given her for Christmas, and a printed jumper. She had changed noticeably since she started school. Her blonde curls were getting a little darker; she seemed more grown-up, and from a fearless, wild four-year-old she had become a gregarious, cheerful five-year-old who kept her own counsel.

She had informed us, while watching the several images of "Mr. Rogers' Neighborhood", which she had once liked, on television, that Mr. Rogers was not talking to her, Anna, but was rather talking to himself. She told us that hair did not grow as long as that of Rapunzel in the fairy tale, but only as long as that of Peggy, the former neighbor, whom she adored.

Her comments, often piercing, had grown more laconic. At age three, she had given me a shocking reflection of myself when I found her posing in front of a mirror, saying "Don't you love me any more?" A real Sarah Bernhardt imitation. But at age five, she deposited a dead bird into the lap of the new landlord, Lindsay Mickles, without a word. If it was his place, it was his bird.

She gave away most of her Christmas presents, we later surmised while trying to find them, keeping only a few things, a record player which she especially liked, and a recording of the Beatles singing "Here Comes the Sun." However, this was not an unusual thing for Anna, who loved giving things away as much as she loved getting them. When she was three, on the first Halloween she was allowed to go Trick-or-Treating with her brothers, she went around the neighborhood, gathering treats, and then sat at the front door the rest of the evening and gave them all away to other Trick-or-Treaters.

On this January day, she greeted the company, checked the soup on the kitchen stove, then changed into blue jeans, her oversized rubber boots, and a blue and white striped tee shirt.

At about 12:40, Anna's friend Becky telephoned from Martin's Beach to arrange for a visit the next day after school. Anna talked to her, laughing, pulling on her brother's leopard-print terrycloth robe.

"If you're going outside, wear a real coat," I said. "Put on your red coat."

Our neighbor Suzanne came in about 1:30, parking her rubber boots at the back door. She sat on the floor in front of the fireplace, her knees drawn up under a long purple skirt. We were talking about Hulk, the rooster.

"Well, I was getting afraid of him myself."

"I know. Every time I'd run into him at the chicken coop, he would try to get behind me."

"He just about scared the life out of me when he flew up on my neck last week."

"Well, he flew at the wrong person this time."

"Wrung his neck, you say?"

Arlene, Asya and their baby left and Suzanne walked up to the road to get her previous day's mail. Some time between 1:30 and 2:00, Anna slipped off the red coat, left it on a stool in the kitchen, and wandered into the glassed-in porch Joe and I used for a bedroom. I heard her talking at about 2:00, perhaps to the cats.

At 2:10, Craig Barrick, a carpenter friend whose work had also been stymied by the rain, arrived. Between 2:15 and 2:20, I became suddenly alarmed because the sounds I had been monitoring, of Anna talking, then opening and closing the back door, then playing in the yard, had stopped.

"Something's wrong," I said. I crossed the back bedroom, opened the door.

"Anna?" There was no answer. Quickly I looked about the back yard, down the path toward Suzanne's house. Nothing. "Anna!" I shouted. Nothing. "Anna, where are you? Answer me!"

Hearing the panic in my voice, Joe and Suzanne appeared on the porch.   "What's the matter?"

"She doesn't answer."

I walked straight down the farm road, Craig and Suzanne behind me, cut through the yard of the Queen Anne and walked across the small footbridge while Craig and Suzanne walked toward the mill on the other side of the large bridge. We met on the bridge, panic in our faces.

"Could she have gone to check for eggs?"

"I'll go down. You look around here. Look at Peggy's house."

"There's nobody there."

"Maybe she forgot."

"I saw her as I came in the front door," Craig said. "I said hello to her. She was in front of the house."

"Maybe she went to get the mail," Suzanne said. "Maybe she saw me opening my mail and didn't know it was from yesterday."

When we looked at the creek, a feeling like an electrical shock started in my head and traveled down to my feet. Normally mild and meandering, the creek now looked like a small river, brown and rushing.

"You don't think she could have come down here?"

"She wouldn't come to the creek by herself."

"Do you think she heard us talking about the rooster? Do you think she could have come down to look for the rooster?"

"Look there. Could those be her footprints on the bank?"

"I think those are mine," Suzanne said. "We were just here. Remember, she and I were trading boots?"

"I'm going back up to the road," I said. "Craig, you saw her as you were coming in?"

"Yes."

"Did you see any cars or anything up on the road?"

"I stopped down the road a bit., you know, west, before I got here. I got out to pet the horses. There was a panel truck, a youngish driver and an older passenger, driving toward the ocean. I thought they were mighty friendly for strangers. But nothing really weird."

I turned back toward the houses. I seemed to hear music coming from Suzanne's house. Songs of the Humpback Whale. Anna liked that record. I ran back up the hill to Suzanne's house, but Anna was not there and there was no music, though I would have sworn that I heard whale sounds. My head was on fire. My legs were like rubber. Running up the hill was like trying to run against deep water. It took forever. I stood there and scanned, like a spotlight, from the road, down across the meadow, past the big barn, past the small barn with the water wheel, over the creek, to the horse barn, across the bridge, across the willows bordering the creek, up the slope, back to where I stood. Nothing.

Then Joe was standing beside me. His face seemed all cracked and broken. "She's gone," he said.

"No!" I screamed. I screamed it with all my breath. I could feel the breath leave me in stages, at first freely, then only with effort, and finally as if I were wringing the last breath out of my chest the way one would wring water from a towel. One word, but I screamed it so long and so loudly that, up and down Purisima Canyon, neighbors on farms a mile away heard that word and dropped whatever they were doing. It was as if that one word had torn the very cloth of time itself.

(Anna, January, 1973, at the old outhouse; last known photo of her)

CHAPTER FOUR

At 3:15 P.M., the San Mateo County Sheriff's deputies arrived. They drove down the farm road and across the bridge and put on their siren, saying that maybe Anna would hear it. Shortly afterward, Nonda and Eddie arrived home from school. "What's going on?"

Helicopters flew up and down the length of the creek, all the way to the Pacific Ocean and back up the hill to Bald Knob. Divers in wetsuits began to explore the creek. Neighbors, having heard the siren, came to the house and then began to search. Charlene Machado, a neighbor who was feeding her horses in a corral east of the Farm on Purisima, said she had heard the siren and then noticed a crackling sound along the creek in a place where there were no animals.

"My first thought was that someone was stealing something," she said.

At dusk, the searchers gathered back at the house. "We can't see anything," they said. "We'll be back at daybreak."

The telephone was dead. The storm had caused a power outage in Half Moon Bay, and apparently had taken down the rural phone line as well. "Call this number for me," I asked the deputies. "It's a doctor friend. Ask if he can send me a sedative."

In only as long as it took to drive from San Francisco, George Stewart and his wife Poki arrived. "I brought pills," he said, "but I don't want you to take them. We'll stay here with you for a few days and help you look for her. Try to do without the pills. I know it's hard. Lie down. See if you can sleep. We'll answer the phone if they get the line repaired."

I lay on the uncomfortable bed, looking at the bamboo blinds as if I could see out into the night. In my mind, I retraced the possible paths she might have taken in the twenty or thirty minutes she was out of my sight. She could have gone up to the mailbox. She could have gone to the chicken coop. She could have gone down to the creek. She could be dead. Someone could have kidnapped her.

My only sense was that there was a great silence, beginning with that moment when it became too quiet. I could imagine but not recall the shriek of the siren or the other noises the siren gathered: agitated voices, cars, the school bus, the barking of our young dog as he followed this person and that person, Saturn with his worried eyes. In memory, there was only the silence and the scraps of low conversation. "Those prints, could they be hers?" Suzanne, saying "I think they're mine." Joe's voice, saying, unbelievably, that she was gone.

Poki touched me on the arm. "There are television people at the door. Can you come talk to them?"

"I can't."

"I'll tell them you can't."

The weather was clear and warm throughout the night. A car patrolled the road from the beach to the house. I lay in bed with my eyes open and felt grateful that at least it was warm, and Anna out there somewhere with no coat.

Some time before dawn, I fell asleep and dreamed of Anna taking wood from the wood bin. I remembered that we had promised to take wood for a carpentry project to the kindergarten class that day, Wednesday. I made a mental note to remember to take the wood to her school.

CHAPTER FIVE

January 17, 1973

At eight-thirty in the morning, sheriff's deputies brought their canine unit. They asked for some item of Anna's clothing that might have perspiration on it, and I gave them a fluffy houseslipper of hers, an orange scuff, well worn, which matched a bathrobe she wore when she wasn't wearing Nonda's threadbare leopard print terry cloth. The tracking dog crawled under a fence at the bridge and went to the creek's edge, the way our dog Saturn often went to drink water, but then the bloodhound doubled back along the bank upstream before quitting.

The owner of the dog said that this was inconclusive. He said they were lucky to get a scent in dry weather, on dry ground, when a trail was only a few hours old; by this time it was 18 or 19 hours after Anna had disappeared, the ground was wet and had been walked on by many searchers.

Two busloads of youth camp volunteers, people from the Forestry Service, divers and helicopter pilots searched the creek, the hillside, and the neighborhood all day.

In the midst of this, Joe said "I don't know what she did, but if she knew it was going to get this much juice, she'd probably do it again."

We sent telegrams to the grandparents and godparents: We ask your prayers for our Anna, who is feared lost here. Intensive search in progress since yesterday.
Love.

George and Poki, who had moved in with us temporarily, went shopping for groceries and made meals. The kitchen was full of salads and casseroles and homemade apple juice brought by the neighbors and by the members of our food club.

It was cold after the sun went down, and the wind blew fiercely all night.

January 18, 1973

Today volunteer divers searched the creek again. I have no intuition at all as to whether she could have gone there or somewhere else. Inside my mind, it is as silent as it was on Tuesday when first I knew something was wrong. I deliberately led everyone to the creek first. In the blazing immediacy of the search, I saw the creek as the most immediate danger. Searching other places could come later, but first it had to be the creek.

Some people came from the Society of Friends Palo Alto meeting at my request. They sat uncomfortably on the piano bench and the couch while I sat in the bean bag chair. They said they remembered seeing me with Anna at a meeting, and how I held her hand. They said that in the old days, people lost children so often that sometimes they would only give them numbers for names, Primus, Decimus, Tertius and so forth, so that they wouldn't become too attached.

Some bikers in old cars came to the house to ask permission to search upstream and over Higgins Canyon Road.

Every time the phone rings, I pick it up and can hear a click or two or three. Is it neighbors on the party line? Are our telephones being monitored? I mentioned this to one of the sheriff's deputies and all he said was "I'm not surprised."

Western Union, Yucaipa, California, Jan. 18, 1973

ALL OUR HOPES AND PRAYERS ARE WITH YOU AND ANNA. PHIL, LIA (Anna's godparents)

Half Moon Bay High School, Jan. 18, 1973

Sympathy card to Nonda, signed by members of the high school band: William MacSems, director; Emily Knox, Allen J. Carlson, Mike Cotruvo, Dan Marcus, Wayne Goodman, Brian Carlson, Peter Sirret, Ken McBride, Al Lander, Randy Remillong, Shannon Gerardo, Ken Wasserman, Virginia LoVette, Erin Sullivan, Darla Mahan, Lisa Hallock, Valerie Lopez, Dave Jackson, Sandie Albert, Ted Avazian, Nancy Lampros, Rick Abbot, Sandy Hardman, Siste Crudel, Martin Partlan, Maile Albert, Allan Calderon, Jim Newell, Kevin Clay, David Squires, Jannette West, Geri Wilson, Paul Johnson, Brian Wright and Keith Remilong.

January 19, 1973

Today I thought I should prepare in case she was dead. While the divers and pilots were searching the creek and the hillside, I made some telephone calls, trying to find out how to get permission to bury her in the old Purisima Cemetery, if in fact we found her body. I went to the fabric store on Main Street to find cloth to make into a burial dress. I bought red velvet and white eyelet. I took the pretty fabric home and tried to make it into a dress, but stopped right in the middle of a seam, turned the sewing machine off and walked away with the red velvet just sitting there under the feed dog.

When I was waiting for her to be born, I sewed little vests, knitted a yellow sweater. When she was an infant, I made her a green velvet dress. I made a doll with green skin, so she would be interested in the varieties of skin color, and a purple velvet whale, Moby Grape. For her first birthday, Joe and I made a horse covered with fake fur. When she was three, I made a green corduroy poncho and a hat to match and she wore it all the time. There was a little Victorian dress I made for her so many times that the pattern fell apart.

The Purisima Cemetery is on the right as you turn off Highway One to Purisima Creek Road. It is strangled by vines and bushes, and nobody has been buried there for years. In the Nineteenth Century, a small town called Purisima sprang up near the creek for which it was named. The town had a school house, a general store, hotel, saloon and dance hall. In 1868 a man named John Purcell deeded the town the cemetery at the corner of Purisima Creek Road and Verde Road.

The death of some of the town's founders, foreclosures and competitions with Spanishtown (Half Moon Bay) all contributed to the demise of the town of Purisima.

We did receive permission to bury Anna in the Purisima Cemetery, should it prove that she had died; she would have been the last person to rest there. But of course we never found anything to bury.

The Irish have wakes so that they might sit with the dead, but we have no rituals for addressing the dead. The Tibetan Book of the Dead, however, has a kind of guide book, not sad or depressing at all, with which one may address the spirit. In case she had gone into the creek, I went down near the bridge and read:

Humbly I honor all you Saints, Teachers, and Great Ones, and ask that you grant liberation to this spirit.

(After offering worship to the Trinity and prayers asking for the help of the Great Ones and the Saints, call the deceased by name three or seven times, and say): O nobly-born, listen to me: When you awoke from your faint, a bright body resembling your former self must have appeared, having senses and the ability to move without limits, but visible only to the eyes of the enlightened.

Depending on where you are to be reborn, you will see images, but do not respond to them. If you cannot resist them, you will be caused to roam about in pain.

If you hold fast to the Truth, you will gain liberation without having to be born again.

We can't seem to find any clues at all, no matter how hard we look. A chickadee flew into the big front window and dropped, dead, onto the ground outside. For lack of other evidence, I wondered if this could be some kind of sign.

Jan. 19, 1973

"If telepathy were a reality you would know that I have been in touch with all of you many times since George Stewart's phone call on

Wednesday afternoon. My heart bleeds for you as you try to face this crisis in your lives. Many prayers have gone out for Anna's safety and for courage and fortitude for all of you. We feel so helpless at this distance but we can pray and are doing so.

"I mailed Eddie a birthday card today which I had prepared before we heard about Anna being lost and that is why there is no mention in it of your problems. I didn't want you to think I was just being callous.

"Please thank George for his phone call and for the calm way he related the circumstances. I couldn't make much of a reply as I was on the main desk when I answered and that is just like talking in public. He and Poki have been such very good friends of yours.

"Much love, Ann" (Anna's paternal Grandmother)

January 20, 1973

Today police divers searched the creek, starting at the ocean and winding up at the house. They said they didn't think they had left anything to check, that they had looked everywhere they could.

I went with George S. to the sheriff's offices in Redwood City, and we talked to Sergeant Brendan Maguire, who asked questions about Anna's father.

Craig, Suzanne, Joe and I put together a chronology of Tuesday, where we were, what we were doing, what we saw, what time we called the sheriff. We thought it was amazing that they actually came to the farm immediately when she had only been unaccounted-for a few minutes, 20 minutes to a half-hour.

Prasadam in Hindi means grace in the form of a gift. Mrs. Scheilein, who was our neighbor in San Francisco before we moved to the farm, came to the house. "Why couldn't it have been me?" she asked. She reminded us of Anna's long "LoLoLo" letters to her friends. After Scheilein left, we found a LoLoLo letter written with black marker on the bathroom cabinet.

At night I dreamed of Anna. She was wearing a brown poncho and looking perplexed. Her hair had just been washed.

New York, N.Y., Jan. 20, 1973

"My folks just called us last night with the terrible news. I guess there's not much I can say that would be any consolation to you--or that would adequately convey how I feel either. I've been thinking of little else since they called, and keep hoping it's not true. Mostly, I wish there were something I could do, but I feel rather helpless. My folks promised to keep us informed of any news, but if there is any way at all in which we can help, please call on us. In the meantime we'll just keep hoping.

"A warm embrace to you all.

Mary-Alice" (Anna's paternal aunt)

January 21, 1973

I finally found the Pinocchio book Anna had borrowed from the Half Moon Bay library. It was under my side of the bed.

John and his brother Ernie came with diving suits to search the creek. Since it had been John who would retrace the water lines whenever our taps went dry, I figure he knew as much about the water situation around Purisima as anyone. Plus the fact that he and Ernie, the sons of a fisherman, probably spent more time in the water than on the land. Joe put on a wetsuit, too, and looked with them while Nonda, Bill and Asya looked along the banks.

Joe found the corpse of Hulk, the rooster, about three quarters of a mile downstream, three feet above the creek's high water line in the brambles. They also found a sock, and we compared it to Anna's socks, but it was too big and not the kind she had been wearing.

Cookeville, Tennessee, Jan. 21, 1973

"It's hard to put the appropriate things in writing. Just know that our thoughts and prayers are with you and that we want to do anything we can.

"Love, Dan" (Anna's maternal uncle)

January 22, 1973

Joe and I searched along the banks of the creek, the bridges, meadows, and the banks upstream, toward Hatch Woods. We drove slowly down Purisima Creek Road, following it into Higgins Canyon Road, then parked the truck high up and looked down on the farm with binoculars. We discovered that there are several places on Higgins where the houses and meadows of our farm may be observed without the watcher being seen. A person could even drive from Half Moon Bay, using this road and not Purisima, and see everything that might be going on around our house without having his vehicle seen near Purisima Creek Road.

We called Bruce Coggins, the blacksmith, to see if he had noticed anything unusual the morning of January 16, when he came to shoe the horses.

Lyndon Johnson died today.

January 23, 1973

I have this recurring dream that it is Christmas again, even though it was Christmas just a few weeks ago. Wearily, I try to find the boxes of decorations and the lights for the Christmas tree which stands outside next to the garbage can with a few strands of tinsel still hanging from it. I drag the tree inside the house and fling the strands of light over it. In a moderate panic, I think that I have forgotten to send cards and gifts.

I can't even remember Christmas, though it was only a month ago. A few days ago a chickadee flew into the front window and killed itself. Today another chickadee flew into the window at an angle, bumped itself but did not break anything and flew away as assuredly as it had flown into the obstacle, or toward the mirrored chickadee or whatever. Anna could have died, or she could still be alive.

There is a truce in Vietnam, an end to the war we have all opposed with such vigor all these years.

Joe and Robert Freeman (from the Food Club) in wetsuits searched Purisima Creek again and were joined by several off-duty men from the Sheriff's office. The water is running low and clear.

January 24, 1973

The afternoon Anna was born, Phil, our neurosurgeon-
drummer friend, appeared at the door of the delivery room at UCSF
while I was still on the table with the baby in my arms. His office and
practice were on a different floor from the Obstetrics suites.

"How can you be here?" I asked. "You never come to this
floor. How did you know we were here?"

"I don't know," he said. "I just had a feeling."

After her father left home, we wanted somehow to have her
baptized, but none of the places we telephoned really wanted to do it.
They didn't know us, and they didn't much like the idea that we
wanted a baby baptized without having to join their churches. So we
more or less did it ourselves, on her first birthday, with Phil and his
wife Lia standing reassuringly by.

Phil has a wonderful smile, curly dark hair and a distinguished
nose. Somehow, with hands the size of hams, he operates on blood
vessels so tiny he has to use a microscope to see them. He was at
Princeton with Anna's father. When we came to San Francisco,
Nonda asked him for drum lessons, and after that, the two of them
would sit for hours, doing flamacues and ratamacues on a big desklike
practice pad they had built.

Today Phil and I made a list of all the search activities we
knew of, the volunteer groups and individuals, who they were and
where they had looked. We took the list to Sergeant Brendan Maguire
in Redwood City.

Joe, Asya, Byron from the Palace Ranch, and Gene from the
food club searched the creek around the treehouse.

CHAPTER SIX

On January 25, 1973, the Half Moon Bay Review ran a story with the headline
GIRL, 5, STILL MISSING IN PURISIMA CANYON AFTER INTENSIVE SEARCH.

The Review referred to the "little blonde, blue-eyed girl" (even though Anna's eyes were brown) as the focus of "the greatest search in coastside history." "Fears were expressed that she may have drowned," the Review said.

The article referred to more than a hundred off-duty sheriff's deputies, Sheriff's Honor Camp inmates, Division of Forestry workers, youth volunteers, divers and neighbors who searched in "the rugged Purisima Creek canyon...where Anna wandered away from her home Tuesday afternoon January 16."

"It's most likely she fell into Purisima Creek," said Eugene Stewart, San Mateo Assistant Sheriff. "But we haven't given up hope."

Shivering in 40 degree weather, four scuba divers, members of the sheriff's reserve, probed every pool and eddy along three miles of the storm swollen creek between the girl's home and a point where the stream empties into the Pacific.

"It's a slow process," said wet suited Sgt. Robert Lauffer, as he paused for a cup of coffee about midway through the search. "I'm 90 per cent sure we didn't miss her, if she's in the creek."

The little girl may have slipped on the muddy stream bank, reports said.

Sheriff's Captain Herbert E. Elvander said that the child... "might never be found."

Elvander said search operations have been suspended "until the creek falls."

More than 100 deputies, Sheriff's Honor Camp inmates, Division of Forestry workers, youth volunteers and neighbors conducted an intensive search in and around the rugged creek.

The captain said the creek was searched along a four-mile course to the ocean. He said searchers broke up log jams and waded and swam in the creek in an effort to find the girl.

"In my opinion," he said, "she might never be found. She might be caught under debris in a cut bank and silted over. We can dig up two miles of creek bottom."

Elvander said the child's pet dog kept running back and forth between the house and the creek, after (her mother) noticed her daughter was missing from the back yard.

Sheriff's canine corps dogs traced the girl to the creek, and her footprints were found there, Elvander said.

"If she fell in that creek, she probably never got out," the captain said. "We had to use rope to pull out our scuba divers, and they're strong swimmers wearing wetsuits."

Reports that the child had a pet rooster and was hunting for it were denied by a source close to the family. She said the child had no pet rooster and was not looking for it in the creek when she disappeared.

It was asserted, however, that there was a rooster in the area that attacked a blacksmith. He became angry and killed the bird and hurled the carcass into the creek. The rooster's body came to the surface on Monday. The child did not witness the rooster killing.

People do not really like a mystery unless they can look at the last chapter and see how it comes out. They like to form an opinion about things early on, and the newspaper was no exception. Using the passive voice to attribute statements from family members, the Half Moon Bay Review, a weekly newspaper whose voice was somewhat belligerent in the days of the legendary editor Ed Bauer, implied that it knew something we didn't about what happened to Anna.

It used a photograph of Anna, but got the color of her eyes wrong, misquoted the authorities, and sought for some sinister connection between Anna's disappearance and the death of the maverick rooster which was no more her pet than were the other chickens of the flock. The newspaper attributed some significance to the fact that her brother's dog ran back and forth between the house and the creek, following the strangers, several days after Anna's disappearance. Saturn had some good qualities, but prescience and brilliance were not among them.

The newspaper's implication that the hapless blacksmith who killed the rooster was somehow responsible for Anna's disappearance no doubt caused that poor man a great deal of grief, and the newspaper's strong bias that Anna had gone into the creek probably kept a number of people from searching for her on the land.

The reporter sensed something strange somewhere. What he did not know, because we did not tell him, was that Sergeant Brendan

Maguire, who would later be elected San Mateo County's sheriff, was at that moment conducting in person an investigation of Anna's father.

Describing George Waters to my sister-in-law, I said "He was brilliant, handsome, poetic."

"A god, in other words," she said.

George Henry Waters II was born April 14, 1939 in Iloilo, Philippines, where his parents, a nurse and a physician, were medical missionaries. He spent some of his early years in a Japanese concentration camp. The fact that his mother was pregnant with his younger sister probably saved the family's lives. The mother was unable to join a group of captives who tried to escape and who were killed by their captors. The family was not abused, but they suffered from serious malnutrition. The younger sister was born in the camp.

After the camp was liberated by United States Marines (curiously, one of them was copy chief on a newspaper where I worked in the early 1960s), George, his older brother and younger sister spent some time at a home for missionary children while their parents returned to work in the Philippines.

George went to the Taft School, a boarding preparatory school in Watertown, Connecticut, whose motto was "not to be served, but to serve" some time between 1953 and 1958. He won the Harvard award, but chose instead to go Princeton, where he played lacrosse, was president of the University Cottage Club, was elected to an academic honor society. He did tutorials with Edmund Keeley, an English professor with many connections to Greece. (Keeley's translations of the poet Odysseus Elytis contributed to the poet's winning the Nobel Prize in 1979.)

Keeley recommended George for a year's job teaching English at the American Farm School in Thessaloniki, and though he had been accepted at Columbia University College of Physicians and Surgeons, George took a year's leave in order to go to Thessaloniki. He graduated cum laude from Princeton in June of 1961.

He was only 22 years old when we met at the American Farm School in Thessaloniki, where I was working and living with my two little boys. He had just climbed the Jungfrau in Switzerland. He had the year planned. He would learn Greek, would reread the Victorian poets, especially Keats, Shelley and Byron, would go to Egypt at Christmas, would leave in June and go to Columbia.

He was tall, slender, brown-eyed. There was something serious and pondering about his gaze, something tentative and vulnerable about the way he stood with his weight on one leg.

In the small resident community of the Farm School, we saw each other every day. I lived with the boys and my husband, Antonios Trimis, in a two-story stone house which still had cleat marks from the days of the German occupation. I occasionally taught a recreation class at the Farm School; I wrote letters and stories and handled correspondence regarding scholarships.

(George Waters, circa 1964)

One day a week, I taught music at Pinewood School, the school for children of consular officials, Voice of America employees, and other foreign dependents. George taught English at Pinewood as well as at the American Farm School. He had a room in the Farm School's single-faculty dormitories.

At the end of the school year, we said goodbye, but it was not easy. George, on his way to New York, turned around in Florence and flew back to northern Greece for an hour of conversation.

When we next met, George was attending medical school in New York City and I was back at my old job at the Knoxville News-Sentinel in Tennessee. I had started as a copy girl after my first year in college and continued through the newspaper hierarchy of that time: television listings, public records, the morgue or newspaper library; the women's department, a weekly column, and finally, reporter. This time I was promoted to the copy desk, a U-shaped affair with the copy chief sitting in the middle and the editors or rim rats around the outside. At journeyman wages, I made enough to rent a shabby studio apartment, buy groceries, and pay for an elaborate sequence of baby-sitters.

Somewhere in all this was Paris. George and I agreed to meet beneath the Winged Victory in the Louvre. If we never saw each other again, at least we would have this time which we called the time between two freedoms. The ten days was not as romantic as we had thought it would be. I was pregnant and sick.

But we went to the Louvre, had a picnic in the Bois de Boulogne, danced in the middle of the night in Les Halles, the old central market, where farmers brought their produce at one or two in the morning; we ate onion soup and listened to accordion music. We tried to ignore the skeptical glances of the farmers and the barely disguised wrath of the hotel concierge, who had to wake up at four in the morning to let us in. We parted, not expecting to meet again. I lost the baby, probably because I had been eating some over-the-counter Greek pills which a pharmacist assured me would bring on the monthly cycle.

In the summer of 1963, George went to Mexico with two old Princeton classmates. I received a civil divorce, not without great protest from my unwilling husband in Greece and from my reluctant lawyer, who referred scathingly to "Hero" (George) and the permanent bulge his pocket edition of Keats made in his pants. I petitioned for and obtained a canonical dissolution from the Greek Orthodox Church. I juggled baby-sitters and swing shifts on the newspaper, tried to learn how to raise my two-year-old and five-year-old boys without the nanny we had always had in Greece.

I cried when the children were asleep. Late one afternoon, after the fifth deadline, the news editor at the paper received word that a figure in a political scandal of the time was visiting her parents in Tennessee for Christmas. All the reporters had gone home. Would I, a copy editor, go with a photographer and try to talk to her?

The story was picked up by the wire services and Newsweek, with my byline. On the strength of this, I took a bus to New York and applied for a job on the New York Herald-Tribune. Virtually assured by managing editor Murray Weiss of a job as the Tribune's first lady copy editor, I gave notice at the News-Sentinel, packed up the trunks and suitcases, and moved with the boys to New York.

A newspaper strike began, the Herald-Tribune had a hiring freeze, I looked everywhere for a writing job. In March, 1964, on Greek Independence Day, George and I were married at the Manhattan

Municipal Building by a justice of the peace who had had elocution lessons and who nasalized every consonant: "Ndearly nbeloved, we are ngathered here..." We tried not to laugh.

George's parents couldn't have been thrilled at his marrying a divorcee with two children, but they were kindly and supportive, visiting us at our apartment and sending presents to the boys.

We bribed our way into a huge rent-controlled apartment on Riverside Drive with a view of the Hudson River from the bathroom, which was decorated in Princeton colors, orange and black. (We gave the superintendent a television set.) The children roller-skated and rode their tricycles down the 40-foot hallway, we shook our Greek rugs down the fire escape, we furnished the place with castoff furniture gleaned from the curb on Wednesday mornings, when unwanted furniture was put out for trash collection.

There were no other children at the medical school, so Nonda and Eddie were the class pets, obligingly coming down with measles when the class was studying childhood diseases (students came to the house to look down their throats for Koplik's Spots), and with pinworms when the students were studying parasitology. Classmates would borrow the children to go snowboarding or to fly radio-controlled airplanes.

Surgical knots were practiced on our dish drainer. Our neighbors down Riverside Drive included a student doctor who has since won the Nobel Prize for Medicine. "If anything happens to you and George," Nonda told me, "We'll go live with Harold and the other George." Another classmate was Robin Cook, the writer of so many medical mysteries.

I found a writing job with a United Nations delegation. George studied, rotated through hospitals throughout New York City, sold blood, worked horrible jobs when he could find them. The worst was one where he sewed up corpses after autopsies. He asked his father if he had any objection to his, George's, selling semen to the fertility clinic. His father replied that as far as he was concerned, the more family genes in the pool, the better.

Every Friday, I split my paycheck evenly with Kay, the baby-sitter who took a bus from the Bronx to uptown Manhattan. Nonda went to Public School 128 on Broadway. Eddie tagged after Kay all day.

I wrote an article about the trials of being married to a medical student whom I rarely saw, and it was published in a magazine called "MD's Wife".

We went to the Cloisters on weekends and to the Museum of Modern Art for painting lessons. George was a conscientious stepfather, making sure the boys brushed their teeth, ordering nonfat milk for Ed because he had the body type which might put on weight or develop cholesterol problems later in life. We went to movies, took day trips to Montauk and Princeton, visited friends whenever we had a few hours together.

Whether he was, as he said, remorseful about taking the children away from their father, or whether family life was simply more than he had bargained for, by June, three months after our wedding, George had applied for and received an elective to study goiter in Euboeia, Greece. In 1966, Tony, the boys' father, said that he had been driving by Alexandras Clinic in Athens, where Nonda was born, and had seen George standing on the steps. "I had several thoughts," Tony said. "One of them was that I would kill him."

At any rate, it was a long summer. At the end of it, George returned, we began marriage counseling, I was promoted to editor at my job. We got through the last year of medical school, sold the windfall furniture, packed everything into a new Volkswagen station wagon which was a graduation present from George's parents, and camped our way across the country to San Francisco, where George had received the internship he most wanted, at San Francisco General Hospital. I turned 30 in the Rockies.

We camped on Mount Tamalpais while we were looking for a permanent place to live. We found a two-bedroom house on Bernal Hill which rented for $150 a month, exactly what we had paid for our enormous rent-controlled apartment in New York with the view of the Hudson River.

If I saw little of George while he was in medical school, I saw even less of him once the internship began. We were referred to another counselor. George took LSD, which was not yet illegal. Notes from my journal of October 9, 1966 describe in somewhat clinical terms his reaction to 700 micrograms of LSD-25 (Owsley's): Uncontrollable trembling of jaw and inner thigh, but not hands. Pulse rate increases, along with body temperature. Some mottling of skin. Subject weeps, says "I was just born". After 12 hours, "marked progress from passive-aggressive fear-dominated reactions of 20 years' duration. External reactions resembling auto-hypnosis, but along with drug-induced psychoses: paranoia (police, death of self, family, friends.) Fear of "letting go", i.e., insanity, actual and apparent, while generally maintaining mental control. Visual memories dating to age one or two. Use of childhood words such as "tata".

November 16, 1965: Weird dream that George's father had a heart attack. The next evening his mother called to say he had had a coronary the previous Thursday, but only just accepted the fact. Meanwhile, we saw a shrink for marriage problems. I made G. some promises, and he reciprocated with the wish to have a baby, completely unexpected, almost frightening.

George applied for Conscientious Objector status with his local draft board in Dundee, New York. We had strong objections to the war in Vietnam, as did most of our friends. We sought advice from the American Friends Service Committee. One-war conscientious objectors had not had much success attaining CO status. George applied for a position with the Public Health department which would have exempted him from the draft, but was refused.

In April, Nonda, age nine, was interviewed on the radio during a peace march.

> *Newsman: What are you doing, son?*
> *Nonda: Marching (waving peace flag.)*
> *Newsman: What is this march? An Easter march? A Christmas march?*
> *Nonda: It's a march for ending the war.*
> *Newsman: What war?*
> *Nonda: The war in Vietnam.*
> *Newsman: Do you think the march will end the war?*
> *Nonda: No, but it's to show how many people want to end the war. Hundreds of different kinds of people want to end the war.*
> *Newsman: What's your name?*
> *Nonda: Nonda.*
> *Newsman: What kind of name is that? What country did it come from?*
> *Nonda: Greece.*

I became pregnant. George wanted us to join a commune with several bachelors and single women. The word "commune" probably evokes a picture quite the opposite of the luxurious quarters on Alabama Street in San Francisco. Bob Dylan actually sang there for the residents and their guests, and Ursula, who lived there, brought the Dalai Lama to visit. We took the children to see the commune's Christmas tree with real candles, but I did not want to live there.

I wrote to psychiatrist Allen Wheelis, who had written a story, "The Illusionless Man and the Visionary Maid", which I admired. We met, and Dr. Wheelis said that a situational rather than a psychological solution seemed to be required for our marriage problems: That I leave, take a lover, or cease to love. He would not answer Henry's question from the story: "Is this all there is?"

George admitted that pregnant me "turned him off", but he made a handcrafted redwood bed inscribed "with so much love". I wrote "a kind of passionless friendliness seems to be developing here."

In June, the local draft board refused George's application for Conscientious Objector status. In my journal, I quoted Christopher Fry: "Thank God for the time we live in, when flames of evil leap and burn."

The afternoon of September 25, 1967, Anna was born. The birth happened so quickly that the obstetricians, Dr. Orcutt and Dr. Chapler, didn't make it to the hospital on time. "Just give me a pudendal block," I told the resident, "because it's going to tear down there and I don't want to feel the stitches."

The resident prodded me and said "Look!" In a large mirror, I saw a head and shoulders, and then hands, palms together, then arms which opened wide just like a seedling opening to the sun.

In a few days we went back to the house on Winfield Street. Our nurse friend Arlene was taking care of the boys at home. Anna slept in the cradle George had made for her.

I had only been home from the hospital a few days when George had to travel back to Dundee to appeal the draft board's decision. I began hemorrhaging and had to go back to the hospital. Our friend Phil scooped up the baby and drove me. He held her while an emergency room doctor replaced some sutures. She looked like a doll in his big hands.

(Posing in costume for the family Christmas card in 1967: The Beatles' Sergeant Pepper's Lonely Hearts Club Band was our favorite record at the time. George holding baby Anna.)

CHAPTER SEVEN

George's senior paper at Princeton was a treatise on Joseph Conrad's short stories, and one passage had a curious resonance with the next chapter in our lives.

"Night fills the sky, I suggest, in a symbolic reflection of the darkness roused in the narrator's mind as he looks at the pathetic figure of Marlow...The narrator, I believe, sees the tragedy in the story of Marlow, who in failing to recognize 'things as they are' laid himself bare for an experience which would shock him so shudderingly as to destroy his faith in the one thing which makes meaningful a world without moral meaning. Marlow, denying faith in humanity, refuting fidelity among men, does so without recognizing his own responsibility for the conclusion of his experience."

At about this time, George had a patient at San Francisco General Hospital called Margaret Kukoda who had a brain tumor, an astrocytoma. She was operated on, did not recover, and was sent to Laguna Honda Hospital, a long-term care facility run by the City of San Francisco. She had a friend in constant attendance, George Brody or Brodie (whom she called Bobby), who made an impression on George. Soon George Waters was bringing this man to the house and introducing him to his friends.

Much later, in 1982, we would learn more about "Margaret" and George Brody from an acquaintance who had rented an apartment at 1006 Noe Street to them. "Margaret", who was listed in a number of places as a nurse, seems to have also used the name "Mary Kay", possibly because she sold cosmetics for that firm. According to the landlord, Matt Reyburn, the couple had been living on Noe Street since before he bought the house in 1962. Brody moved out shortly after Mary Kay or Margaret died Aug. 3, 1967. Reyburn said that the couple paid their rent in cash, that Brody was "strange", and that he didn't believe he worked anywhere. Brody had power of attorney for Margaret or Mary Kay.

Brody was a man probably in his late seventies, white-haired, with piercing blue eyes behind old-fashioned glasses, with the slightly jutting square jaw one associates with ill-fitting dentures. He wore a suit and tie, an overcoat and a fedora. He claimed to be a Leo, a numerologic 27, an egoist, someone who could read the "akashic records", a person with the ability to change people's lives for the better.

I found Brody somewhat frightening and overbearing and could not understand George's increasing fascination with him, but more often than not, the only times I saw my husband were when he brought Brody to the house. More and more, Brody seemed to be giving George Waters instructions on various matters ranging from dealing with the draft board to exercise and diet.

At first, the suggestions were innocent enough. I was not afraid to leave the children with the two Georges in order to attend a Greek Easter service, and after Anna could take a bottle, I went to southern California by bus to attend the wedding of our friends Wylie, who had succeeded George at the Farm School as the annual Princeton English teacher, and his Judy.

Before long, I would not let the children out of my sight. I caught a cold, and Brody suggested that Anna be brought to his hotel room so that she would not become "contaminated". Brody suggested that the boys should be sent to boarding school because they were too close to me. Calling himself Anna's "godfather without portfolio", he wanted her name changed so that it would be a "numerologic 27" like his own. George Brody said that the name Anna Christian Waters was not sufficiently strong numerologically and that he would change it so that the baby would be a "27". He came up with several possibilities, all of which I refused. I had wanted to name the baby for George's mother and my sister, and the name Anna meant "Grace", which was, well, how I thought of the baby. As a compromise, Brody offered the addition of the name "Eifee" to Anna Christian. I objected, but George Waters said he "did not find the name a bastardization" and proceeded to have Anna's birth certificate amended to include the name. Brody suggested that his friend Margaret might have reincarnated in Anna. Brody referred to Anna as "the tot" and for some reason called me "Gypsy".

In December, 1967, I wrote: Little Anna ... never complains without cause, is content to lie in her cradle and carry on a one-sided conversation with her stuffed dog. George Brody suggested we get her a dog, a light brown poodle.

Journal entry of February, 1968: "I must include last night's absolutely absurd episode. George, apparently suffering from a virus, had been urged by Brody, his mentor, to take a purge, an enema administered by me, lemonade to be taken simultaneously. So picture at 2 A.M. a stringy-haired puffy-eyed me in granny glasses and pink flannel nightgown, mad at the poor victim for something or other involving consideration, holding enema bag which he is applying in the bath, saying "drink your hot lemonade", etc., until everything goes wrong and we finally both dissolve into helpless laughter. Amazing that, at this point, we could still laugh.

The next day's note is less funny: "I am virtually forbidden to talk to anyone. I am beginning to understand better the genius of schizophrenics, who grasp the void and can't get back."

George's friends were not impressed with Brody; in fact, one doctor friend suggested that his "visions" stemmed from a coronary insufficiency. One by one, as George presented his new mentor to his friends, they would behave in some less than satisfactory way and George would formally "sever connections" with them.

March 15, 1968: "impassioned arguments lasting hours, on things such as free will, God, action, destiny, etc. Worse than college sophomores. When George let slip something about Brody being 'more gifted than Jesus', I really flipped. I accused him of not having any priorities or values and of leaning on Brody to make all his decisions. In Greece, I felt as if I were fighting for my life, but now I feel as if I'm fighting for my soul."

When George was away, which was often, the children and I had almost normal lives. The boys went to school; I sewed and kept house and tried to write. I spent a lot of time trying to find some way out of our difficulties. The evenings were something else: Often

George, who had begun to imitate Brody's style of talking and dressing, would show up with him in tow, always carrying a bottle of brandy, which he set on the kitchen table before the harangues began.

When George appeared by himself, it was usually to try to get me to sign some paper or the other having to do with instructions from his mentor. A life insurance policy, an admission of my failings. One tragi-comic scene occurred before the baby was down for the night. She had begun crawling, and we had a kind of expanding lattice gate blocking off the staircase which led down to Winfield Street. In mid-harangue, Anna pushed the gate and actually tobogganed atop it, all the way down the staircase, probably 12 steps and a landing. She was unhurt, didn't even cry, but she effectively put an end to the monologue.

Several times, George traveled some distance just to appear on someone's doorstep, deliver a threat, and leave immediately. Twice he flew to Wisconsin from San Francisco for such a scene at his parents' house. At one point, he forced me into the car and took me on a wild drive--I cannot remember why. Once when Anna had had a febrile convulsion and her pediatrician had prescribed medicine for her, George insisted that she take lemon juice instead of the medicine and left the house when I refused to comply.

I was certain that Brody was dictating the various telegrams, letters and telephone calls George made, asking for money, demanding apologies for imagined insults.

May 15, 1968: After waking me at midnight yesterday--after eight hours with his friend--George informed me that he had told same "never to come or call here again," and for good measure had called our friends the Fines to inform them that they were no longer welcome here, though he was willing to accept Dick's $20,000 for lawyers, etc. So he has barred from the house, bodily or verbally, Jeffrey, Byron, Jerry, Brenda and the Fines. His parents have "failed themselves", and that relationship is strained if not severed (they denied his request for a large loan.) Next in the firing line is Stephen. That will leave only Phil, who still gives Nonda drum lessons. Since George considers him "self-deluded in his marriage" and plans to ask him for $20,000, it remains to be seen whether anyone from the outside world will be allowed here. I protested all this. "We must separate," George said, "immediately, and apply for a divorce on a claim of sexual incompatibility." Even his speech sounds like something which has been learned and rehearsed.

His language became abusive and his ideation seemed so bizarre that it was as if he were possessed. There was a terrible scene on a day when George had promised to take the children to the zoo for a birthday celebration. He came home as promised but said he would only do the zoo trip if I signed the document confessing my transgressions. I refused. Both children were in tears.

I wrote a book of poems, "The Phoenician Sailor", to be sold to raise money for George's Conscientious Objector attempt. UC Med School formed a committee to support George's case, and the book raised about $700. It was well received and was included on some college syllabuses the next year.

George said he was "in love" with the baby, though he rarely saw her and never took her away from the house. She slept in the cradle he had made for her, and when she could sit up, she sat in a redwood baby chair, also made by George, to go with a table and benches for the rest of the family, each with the appropriate astrological sign. He used an old-fashioned draw plane to construct the rustic furniture.

George approached a gay friend, asking if he would write that he had had homosexual relations with him so that the paper could be sent to the draft board in Dundee. He sought a paper from a psychiatrist saying that he was mentally deranged.

And so he began attending sessions with Dr. John Dusay. A medical doctor in private practice in San Francisco, Dr. Dusay had studied transactional analysis with Eric Berne. George hoped to obtain a letter from Dr. Dusay which would exempt him from the draft on the basis of mental illness, but said he would consent to sessions with Dr. Dusay only if I attended, since I was the one who really needed the help, and if his parents paid.

At some point in 1968, my mother, who is afraid of nothing, came to San Francisco to visit and George brought Brody to the house to meet her. She seemed to take an instant dislike to him; I could tell by the icily polite Southern smile, the one which gives away nothing. Finally she said, astonishingly, "I think I have brought my daughter up to be really too nice to everybody. Sometimes you just can't really be nice to everybody."

George's game, Dr. Dusay said, was "Take me as I am", a game nobody could win, since as soon as the other player accepted George's challenge, the ante would be raised. I didn't think summing up George's bizarre behavior as some sort of game adequately described it. There was, however, also a formal diagnosis: Paranoid Schizophrenia, for which few treatment options were successful at that time.

In August, 1968, Dr. Dusay suggested hospitalization for George, whose father and brother flew to San Francisco to discuss the matter with me. Involuntary commitment, however, would result in George's medical license being suspended, and his work as a physician was the closest thing to normal in his life. We couldn't bring ourselves to commit him, and there was no chance at all that he would consent to being hospitalized.

August 28, 1968: G. launched a day-long crusade to get me to admit "you are in love with George Brody." It is preposterous, of course, but George screamed "Our whole marriage depends on your admitting the truth! You don't love me! You don't want me! You only want him. You're in love with him!" Then, in the car, in front of the children, he said "I'm getting out of this marriage. It's the worst possible place I could find myself." After another futile attempt by me to reconcile things, he drove away.

September 3: I dropped my yoga class at the Himalayan Academy today. It's one more bone of contention. George has been out every night the past three weeks until early morning, feigns anger with Brody for "exposing me as an egotist and a liar:", etc., etc., but advises me to "get on your knees and beg George Brody to take a free hand in your life again."

Probably at this point George Waters was living with Brody, though Dr. Dusay said that with George's "problems with intimacy", it was unlikely that he should be living with or even seeing Brody. My brother, Dan, reading these pages in 2006, said that he believed George was really a victim of two wars, World War II, which caused him to be imprisoned in the concentration camp, and the Vietnam war, during which he tried desperately to attain conscientious objector status.

September 8, 1968: George came in at 5:30 this morning. Later in the afternoon, he called me some particularly ugly names and hit me several times.

September 15: After much thought, I "confessed" to all his accusations. By admitting the worst, even if you're not guilty, you can ascertain a margin of innocence. After praising references to Barbra

Streisand, Fritz Kreisler, Caruso and other famous people he connects with George Brody because of numerology or something, he walked happily down the stairs in his new old man's clothes and out, God knows where. I feel utterly betrayed.

September 22: I rescinded the "confessions". I was feeling martyred, and nothing else has changed.

September 27: Anna's birthday (Sept. 25) was a happy event despite everything. Last night, more talk of separation. We have really been separated for more than two months now. He comes home nightly from 12:30 to 5:30 A.M. and sleeps downstairs alone. But for some unexplained reason, he has shown up at 8:30 or so for three nights running.

September 30: I threatened to sue Brody for alienation of affection. So George brought him to the house and I obediently sat up until 3 A.M. hearing about how gifted Brody is, how terribly much George loves him (would die for him, unbounded admiration, his ideal, etc.) and over and over how G. does not love me, is not sexually attracted to me and so on ad nauseum. I mentioned meetings between the two of them and was told "There have been no meetings. We have no relationship. We don't see each other." George glows, beams, smiles. He is rapt with adulation.

October 18: George said that after he asked Brody to refrain from participating in our lives, Brody said such an action would cause me to grow crazy or die. He said George and I wouldn't be together a year from now, and when I cried at this, George was certain that I was crying because I "loved" Brody and was heartbroken that he was leaving. "George Brody held this marriage together all along, even before we met him, and he's still holding it together." This, with the most abusive gutter language imaginable.

November 2: George delivers an ultimatum that I write Brody a letter declaring that I am in love with him and begging him to "come back and hold our marriage together", within 24 hours, or he will leave.

November 3: After going through my pocketbook, appropriating two credit cards and the checkbook, George leaves, carrying his suitcase, leaving me with $20.

November 21: Today there was a ludicrous scene with Gib Kerwin, the lawyer George's brother recommended, tensely waiting outside the bathroom while George took the world's longest shower to avoid coming out (I, nervously chain-smoking, torn between feelings and reason). Finally he emerged, ashen, and Gib served him with a summons to vacate the premises and to refrain from disposing of our community property, etc. That evening George appeared again, promising to stay home more, to be reasonable, etc.

December 3: Sometimes between all these ordeals, we have a normal life. At the height of frolicking to Russian radio music Nonda, wearing an astrakhan, shouts "vodka!" and breaks us up. Ed, regarding his temper, says "It just slides right by me and I can't grab onto it."

January, 1969: George is making the rounds of the somewhat reduced circle of our friends, telling them I'm in love with his self-styled psychic friend and begging them to make me write letters of apology to same.

March 8, 1969: Physical abuse because I will not "make peace" with Brody. I find myself unsympathetic to mental illness.

May 20, 1969, letter from George's father:
"I am enclosing herewith the notarized affidavits you requested concerning the money gifts and the car, and also--with considerable mental reservations--the thousand dollars you requested for the lawyer...I am fearful that you are under some other financial pressure--even amounting to blackmail--which makes it "impossible" for you to immediately terminate your nocturnal absences from home...We just cannot go on dishing out (money) by the hundreds and thousands."

May 25, 1969: Sunday, as George prepares finally to move out, I read Mary Poppins Comes Back: "I am earth and air and fire and water," she (the baby) said softly. "I come from the Dark where all things have their beginning...I come from the sea and its tides,"

Annabel went on. "I come from the sky and its stars, I come from the sun and its brightness..and I come from the forests of earth...Slowly I moved at first, said Annabel, 'Always sleeping and dreaming. I remembered all I had been and I thought of all I shall be. And when I had dreamed my dream I awoke and came swiftly." She paused, her blue eyes full of memories. "And then?" prompted the fledgling. "I heard the stars singing as I came and I felt warm wings about me. I passed the beasts of the jungle and came through the dark, deep waters. It was a long journey." (Mary Poppins Comes Back, by P. L. Travers)

July 20, 1969, letter from George's father:
"I am getting a little bit impatient with your abusive name-calling, and your insistence in blaming everything on Bill and me. Our putting Mikie in touch with Gib (Kerwin, the lawyer) is not the cause of your troubles...when you walked out on her, took all the money, and closed out the bank accounts, leaving her with three small children and no visible means of support--I do not apologize for coming out. And in our interview you gave me no indication of intention, plan or program for improving the situation.

"Then as to finances--As far as the $300 a month as combined alimony and child support...I do not accept any responsibility on that. As I said...it seems to be a light decree, and you will have to budget it out of your income.

"These are my answers to your specific accusations and demands. But beyond this lies a vast field of concern for the failure of your marriage and home life, for the complete change of your personality over the past two years, and for your obvious misery and unhappiness. We do covet for you a good life. With love from us both..."

We were divorced. George insisted on joint custody of Anna. He took an entire roll of pictures of her, but left the negatives and proof sheet with me. He took the car "for sentimental reasons" and agreed to pay $125 a month alimony and $175 a month child support.

CHAPTER EIGHT

January 25, 1973

What a terrible birthday for Eddie. But Suzanne and I discussed it with him and asked if it would be all right to postpone his birthday until February, and then have a birthday party for him closer to Suzanne's birthday.

Sergeant Maguire reports that George is living with his mentor in a hotel downtown in San Francisco. Lindsay Mickles, the landlord, has brought an Airstream trailer to park down near the Queen Anne and reports on his plans for the farm as if nothing had happened here. Joe and I switched houses with Suzanne because she thought we'd get a good night's sleep on her water bed. She says Anna picked the name for Melon, the cat.

January 26, 1973

Sergeant Maguire came to the farm with his superior and stopped Joe as he was about to search the creek again. The three of them drove over Higgins Canyon Road to see the places where someone could have watched the farm to see when the school bus arrived, etc.

January 27, 1973

Today I accompanied the high school chorus to a festival in Stockton. Outside, it probably seems as if I am behaving normally, but inside, all my thoughts flow into the question of where Anna could be and what may have happened to her.

Teachers and chaperones, perhaps twenty of us, were seated in folding chairs on the stage, with the piano. Filling the seats of the auditorium and facing us were some two thousand teenagers from high school choirs all over northern California. Their faces blurred in the half-dark. There was a low hum of conversation and then silence as the conductor lifted his hand. And then the voices. And then the voices. It was like the breath from an enormous organ pipe, followed by an unearthly singing, as if all the angels of heaven were singing consolation and comfort to the two dozen chosen ones seated on the stage.

Every song seemed to have some special message for me. I sat there, afraid to move a muscle lest I wake up at home in my bed. The music went on and on. When intermission came, I wandered out into the halls and found myself surrounded by children who were humming and singing fragments of the choral pieces, as though reminding me of their message.

Some of the singers were wearing buttons which said "Missing In Action, Dead or Alive?" It was as if my question had appeared on their young bosoms, though later I thought maybe the buttons referred to soldiers taken prisoner in Vietnam. The sense of unreality continued throughout the day, underscored by music. On the bus going back to Half Moon Bay, Bill MacSems, the high school music teacher, turned and called me "Mary", though he certainly knows my name. I thought of Michelangelo's Pieta, with Mary bent over the body of her son.

It was difficult being away from the farm all day. I have to make the effort not to be totally obsessed with the search. I cannot sort out my feelings. I suppose the message is that life goes on, that great cliché, but I feel as if I have died or gone mad and am going through the motions of being who I was. Doing me on a cellular level, we would have said in the days we were hippies. Playing a part. The Vietnam peace took place at 3:45 P.M., while the chorus was singing joyful songs.

January 29, 1973

Yesterday all sorts of people were here, Michael S., the horse people. We moved the landlord's Airstream into a place where it isn't quite so visible from the road, this big silver wiener with all its comfortable conveniences. Joe finished reading Zen in the Art of Archery. It rained. Someone from the Sheriff's office checked around the bridge again.

January 31, 1973

We called Sergeant Maguire, who says George and his companion Brody haven't been seen at the hotel for more than a week. My brother Les and his family are coming from Hawaii Friday. They will stay in Lindsay's Airstream, which is parked in the back yard.

Crestwood, Kentucky, Jan. 31, 1973

"Kerry and I just received a letter from Mom and Dad yesterday telling us of the disappearance of little Anna. We are both very concerned about her and Mikie as well. Surely as God takes care of the lilies of the field he'll also watch over little Anna and see she gets back home safely. We are praying for her and for you all.
"Ruth" (a cousin by marriage)

Montara, California, Feb. 1, 1973

"Just wanted to drop you a note to let you know you and your family are in my thoughts and in my prayers. Janice and I would like to come down to see you one afternoon soon--perhaps, next week. We're looking forward to having a cup of your good mint tea. We'll call you before we come.
"Very sincerely, Ruth" (Anna's kindergarten teacher)

Thessaloniki, Greece (no date)

"Your letter, its contents, the thoughts all touched me so--we have been praying, thinking, wishing, hoping ever since Tony told us-- he too is so wrought up about it all, and we so wish there were something, anything we could do to overcome the basic helpless, hopeless feeling of being this far away.
"Every thought, every wish is coming your way and we just wish there were something more positive to do.
"I don't know whether there is any answer beyond love, and you know you have all of that from us which we could possibly send along with our prayers.
"Love to Nonda and Eddie, too. I know how distressed and upset they must be too.
"Affectionately, Bruce" (Lansdale, director of the American Farm School)

Salinas, California, February 1, 1973

"Just received the news of Anna's disappearance today. Our thoughts are happy and the energy here is very positive. We spoke with Gloria on the phone just a minute ago. The three of us would like to come to see all of you very soon. Gloria sends her love.

"I'm still pampering the geranium you gave us--I've been gently insisting that it bloom for quite a while now without success.

"Dayna "

Honolulu, Hawaii, February 1, 1973

"My mother's heart goes out to you. I can't fully grasp the loss of Anna. I'm still mentally searching the farm. I keep calling and sending out energy and it is all cold and echoing. I want to hold you and Joe and the boys and tell you how much we love you and need you.

"I take comfort in Bill's words that Anna had a good life surrounded by good people, and gave joy while here. I look at the picture of her you gave us for Christmas--her gold hair all framed in bright sunshine and her warm face and I feel good inside.

"I cry for you and me and all who loved Anna and now must make ourselves continue, leaving her behind. How terribly hard it is.

"I feel the need to stop and have people stop and observe a time of mourning. Anna has gone from us and we need to voice again how important life is--each individual life.

"I'm sorry we are so very far away in your time of need. I should so much have wanted to search for Anna myself--a need of mine.

"I addressed this to you, Mikie, I guess because every time I tuck (my boys) in each night, I think what it must be like not to tuck them in and I'm glad you have Joe, Nonda and Eddie. I've always admired your strength and staying power, Mikie. I hope, with a little help from your friends, it holds for you now. We all miss Anna but the mother who helps her get the knots out of the shoelaces and gets the peanut butter off the top shelf for her and hurries her so she won't miss the bus to school is going to miss her most of all. I wish there

were some way I could take some of your pain and hold it for you. I reach out my hand, Mikie.

"*Love, Laana*" (Anna's aunt)

Salinas, California, February 4, 1973

"*I've intended to call ever since Gloria passed the news on to me, but invariably, every time I'd reach for the phone I'd catch myself doing the worst thing you can do; that god-awful thing of "rehearsing"...and then, not being able to come up with anything 'right' to say, I'd postpone the whole thing...which probably was best, in the long run, anyway.*

"*So, here I am, with so much to say--and nothing to say--and maybe that's best, in the long run, too. Ego to the contrary, I guess there are events and experiences in life that are quite sufficient unto themselves, that don't need to be decorated by our validating expressions.*

"*So...I'll let it be. Big of me, huh?*

"*Being Here and Being Now, I love you, and am very much with you. And, like...what's new with you guys these days?*

"*Onward, Bob* "

Half Moon Bay, California, Feb. 4, 1973

"*I don't have any idea how to write this, but I'm going to try, anyway. Jim and Greg and I are so very sorry about the loss of your little Anna. I feel deep remorse in my heart and I want you to know that I feel warm toward you and wish there was some support I could give you.*

"*Sincerely, Laurel*"

February 5, 1973

Joe went over the creek again and found an unmated sock the right size, but he found it upstream, not downstream, and it didn't look like any of Anna's socks.

Half Moon Bay, California, Feb. 5, 1973

I don't really know what to say except, I'm sorry. Anna must have made up a lot of the family. I'm sorry.
Sincerely, Greg Jernigan

Kingston, Tennessee, February 5, 1973

It was so good to get your letter. We have wanted so much to help you, but instead, you help us by being strong and doing whatever must be done. Our love for you is beyond expression. All of our friends are much concerned about you and pray for Anna's return. My clothes are still packed, and I bought $200 in traveler's checks to be ready to go to California if you needed me. I'm so glad you have friends like Suzanne and George and Poki. If you need any money, please just tell us. We hesitate to send it unless you say it's O.K. We have plenty, so don't do without anything you need.
Love, Mother

Creswell, Oregon, Feb. 5, 1973

Dear friends, our hearts go out to you--love and strength be with you--I share your pain--Amen to life in this world. Cotton and I dug the "Farmer's Feed Book"--you guys have a good scene! I'm into sprouting alfalfa seeds now, in a week I'll be able to sprout 1200 pounds a month I get 85 cents a pound in four-ounce packages--most Eugene markets carry them--we're "Sprout City Sprouts." Cotton and I are also into ASTROLOGY heavy; so send us all your birth dates, times, places!! Mikie, what time zone is Greece in?? When would it be cool for a visit? --Love to you all
Steve

February 6, 1973

My brother Les gave a music class at the high school as a visiting trombone expert. Our lawyer friend W. called and said that George did call his lawyer "about the time the story broke" to find out what the stories of Anna's disappearance meant. It seemed so strange that he would not call or express any interest, even though we thought we maybe saw his VW station wagon up on the road a couple of times. So at least he knows that she is missing.

CHAPTER NINE

February 8, 1973

    The chicks are beginning to hatch under the mother hens in the coop. You can tell by the hens' preoccupied expressions, and the broken shells which they push out of the nests with their beaks.

Thessaloniki, Greece, February 8, 1973

    It is past nine o'clock at night and I am here in my office in front of the office window looking at my geranium plant and listening to beautiful Vivaldi, "The Four Seasons." Your letter and the newspaper clipping is to my right and on my desk a flower pot with a growing tulip plant. The tulip is not in bloom yet.

    I am thinking about all four of you. I have been thinking about you since I received the letter three days ago.

    What can I say?

    Tears came to my eyes when I read the article and the letter. I missed something I saw so little and I loved so much. I left the office and went home. I was determined to say nothing to anyone. Eli asked me why I was so pale and asked if anything had happened to me. In a faint voice I told her about Anna. I left the room because I did not want Antigone and Marina to see me. We went to our bedroom and I told Eli the whole story.

    Three days went by and every single one was a day of thought. I thought of darkness; I thought of light; I thought of color and love. What more can I say?

    Maybe of hope. We should all have hope. Maybe Anna wandered into the wilderness and she was picked up by someone with the intention of protecting her. Maybe Anna will come back soon. I agree with you that being what she is, one way or another she's all right.

    Tony (Nonda and Ed's father)

February 9, 1973

Les, Haidee and Kamalei left for Hawaii. It was good having my brother, his flower-like wife, and their little three-year-old around. They stayed in the Airstream, our temporary guest house, but there was no heat down there and Haidee, used to the balmy temperatures of Hawaii, got a cold.

Detective Maguire reports regularly on his investigation.

February 10, 1973

Maguire revealed a sordid hypothesis regarding his confrontation with Anna's father and his mentor Tuesday. I cannot even bear to talk about it. *(A note from 2007. The suggestion was so terrible to me that I blocked it from my mind and have never been able to remember what it was. The significance of this diary entry, however, was pointed out by my brother Dan. It is the only documented reference to the fact that a law enforcement officer believed that George and George may have been involved in Anna's disappearance.)*

Knoxville, Tennessee, February 10, 1973

We've been thinking about you and hoping and praying for a happy ending to your long vigil. I talked to (your mother) this morning, and she told me you were quite courageous. That's a definite plus. It's always best to keep a positive outlook.

We enjoyed your letter so much--and today, since Harry is having to work (He also has to work tomorrow--there's to be a reduction in force of 700 more--thanks to Pres. Nixon's cutting another million out of their budget), I'm trying to catch up with my letter writing.

I had to write a thank-you letter to a friend from last summer's trip around the world for sending me 200 slides from the tour.

Next, I have to write to my pen pal in Pakistan. His name is Saluddin (only one name). He lives in a fort, and is studying to be a doctor.

Many families in Pakistan, Afghanistan (and possibly other countries) live in forts for protection. As we went through the Khyber

---

Pass, we saw tribesmen patrolling the road. We were told not to take pictures or stop--just to look ahead and keep driving.

It's an area of smugglers. There's much competition between families. Sometimes they try to shoot into each other's forts.

The forts are made of mud, very thick-walled, and with an observation tower. Sometimes as many as 15 families (or one extended family) live in one fort. We went inside one in Afghanistan. The animals were kept there also. Out guide persuaded the grandmother to uncover her face--and I took a Polaroid shot. It was the first time she had seen her picture.

A friend on the tour took her picture as she looked at the picture I took. I now have a slide of that.

Remember, we're pulling for you.

Love, Mimi and Uncle Harry

February 11, 1973

Kenny offered Joe a new job, which is welcome. I have been driving in to San Francisco to work at my old job at Dr. Robinson's office. Every day we deal with the life and death of children here. We treat children who were born with broken hearts, and we try to find out in what way their hearts are wrong, and to make strategies for setting them right.

Anna was with us when I first worked for Dr. Robinson. He hired me because I wrote "usually cheerful" on my application, under the heading of Disposition, which I did not know meant whether the applicant was hired or not. Dr. Robinson said he had to have someone in the office who was usually cheerful; he didn't even care if she could type. Anna, introduced to Dr. Robinson, licked his face like a cat, and he didn't wipe it off, though his eyes got big behind his glasses and he laughed out loud. A great-hearted man, and a saver of many children's lives.

The San Francisco Chronicle called and offered me a writing job two weeks after I started at Dr. Robinson's office. When things did not go well, when we lost a child and Dr. Robinson threw darts at his own photograph, glued to the dart board, I wondered if it wouldn't have been easier to take the job with the Chronicle.

A game I play while taking the histories is to try to guess the diagnosis, and this past week I got a tricky one: Coarctation of the aorta versus a metabolic disturbance. I look at the records of babies born this past year and wonder about reincarnation and all sorts of things. I look for Anna in all possibilities.

The Vietnam prisoners are returning.

February 13, 1973

Today we had visits from all the people who were here the day Anna disappeared, and once again we tried to go over the time sequence and the events. It was as if, by doing so, we disturbed the calm of the entire neighborhood (if you can call Purisima a neighborhood.) All kinds of noise, dogfights, and furor seemed to break out. We waited all day, from nine in the morning to eleven at night, for a call from Detective Maguire. Almost everyone else we know telephoned, but not Maguire.

February 14, 1973

Finally Maguire called at 9:30 this morning. He is giving up the investigation. He doesn't think George and Brody had anything to do with Anna's disappearance, thinks they are involved with each other and with their own version of the way the world works. Although I think their relationship is teacher-student or guru-devotee and that their actions, while eccentric and maybe suspicious, could in no way rule out their involvement, I was unable to convince Maguire otherwise. Profound depression.

(The official case file on Anna shows no activity after this date.)

February 15, 1973

A mysterious letter and tickets to the Royal Shakespeare Company's production of Midsummer Night's Dream arrived in the mail with no return address and no name on it. Nothing is innocent to me. I compared the stamps with those which had been on the check which came from George for Anna last month, went over the tickets and the envelope, trying to see it meant anything. Did it mean she would be returned to us on Midsummer Night, or anything like that?

(The tickets proved to have been sent by George and Poki as a surprise.)

When George was in medical school, I sometimes attended psychology classes at Columbia's College of Physicians and Surgeons, either because George could not be in class and wanted me to take notes, or because he thought it was something in which I would be interested.

One lecture on hypnosis showed, with a nurse subject, how our conscious mind tries to make sense of things. When the nurse could not account for the missing ten minutes she had been in a trance, she suggested all sorts of things: the clock was wrong or had stopped, or that she or the doctor-hypnotist had mistaken the time, rather than consider she had been in an altered state.

I know that schizophrenics, trying to make sense of their world, get what doctors call ideas of reference, where things having little significance to others seem to contain special messages or advice to the subject.

I know I'm doing this. But I have looked everywhere I can think of without a single clue as to what happened to Anna. Maybe the two chickadees, one which flew into the window, one which escaped, really were trying to tell me something. Maybe there is some message in these tickets to the play. Maybe I am schizophrenic. But I think perhaps schizophrenics do not think they are crazy.

Byron Edelen and Stan were here and stayed up talking until very late. At about four in the morning, I got up and talked to Byron until the sun came up.

Menlo Park, California, Feb. 15, 1973
Lindsay has left and has asked me to notify you of a rent change to go into effect before he returns. Due to many things, we regretfully have to increase your rent to $200.00 per month starting the payment for the month of March. You can consider this as permanent, and if there are any questions, please feel free to contact me at any time.
Very truly, Priscilla Gilbert for Lindsay M. Mickles Enterprises

---

February 16, 1973
I got out my old Shakespeare and read "Midsummer Night's Dream" to see if anything jumped out at me.

February 17, 1973
Today the postman, (actually post-woman, Margaret "Bud" Machado) who keeps horses in a pasture near the creek, found

"something" on the banks which turned out to be nothing, and someone suggested consulting a psychic.

We looked at the full moon with our new telescope which we bought at a barn sale.

(No date) 1973, Bodh Gaya, India

Yesterday at 12:15 I was ordained as a novice nun by Ling Rinpoche, the most learned man among the Tibetans...I requested Ling Rinpoche to do a Mo (Tibetan system of divination). And apparently (he) threw it three times and is convinced that Anna is still alive. I tried to ask him for more details, but they say--Tenzin Gyshe, secretary to H.H. (His Holiness)--that detailed information like place names, etc....are not possible. So I made offering and requested Ling Rinpoche and H.H. the Dalai Lama to pray for Anna's well-being wherever she may be. I do hope that H.H. praying for her will relax your mind a little and make you feel good.

Usch

(Ursula (Usch), front row, right, with H. H. the Dalai Lama and other monks .)

February 19, 1973

Our lawyer friend Wylie says he will call Maguire tomorrow and then call us to see if anything at all is going on.

Kingston, Tennessee, February 19, 1973

I turned up something I didn't know in my research. My great aunt Emma (Ruth was named for her) was born in 1857, was divorced (unheard of in those days), and lost a little three-year-old girl almost the same time her father lost a three-year-old boy, having lost his wife the year before. I barely remember Aunt Emma. She must have died 50 years ago.

Love, Mother

February 20, 1973

The landlord sent a hapless woman out to press for the rent increase, and we countered with the fact that this is not the best time to do that. With the condition of this place, shacks tumbling down, fences in disrepair, we cannot rule out Anna's having met with some accident here on the farm, though really we have looked everywhere we can think of to look. Obviously they want us to move, and obviously we cannot move while we are still searching. It reminds me of that Bob Dylan song: "Hey, landlord, please don't put a price on my head."

Suzanne and Stan have gone to Novato and may check out the psychic whose name we were given.

Green Valley, Arizona, Feb. 20, 1973

I keep you in my thoughts and in my prayers every hour of the day. After I got your news I walked and cried--I was simply unable to believe it could have happened. Talking to you brought me some comfort, and I hope that my concern for you and yours brought you some slight lessening of your troubles.

Please call me collect if you have any news. I shall so want to hear from you. I think of you and pray that your ordeal will be ended soon.

With love, Lois Batton (Anna's baby-sitter in San Francisco)

February 25, 1973

At the Friends meeting today people talked about energy, about seeing "through a glass darkly", and about love. Back home, I looked up a hummingbird I saw in the bird book and found that it was called an Anna's Hummingbird. We bought a Suffolk ewe and I named her Anastasia.

February 26, 1973

Eddie, the dog and I were chasing the new ewe when we heard laughter coming from the children's bedroom. Anna had a toy called a "barrel of laughs" and her cat, Lionel, had rolled over on it and made it go off.

March 1, 1973

We got a letter from that psychic in Novato which said Anna was dead. I was wrecked by these words, and when Nonda was late coming back from a track meet, I became hysterical. Finally we went to an elephant movie at Von's Cinema and I fell asleep right there in the dark.

CHAPTER TEN

March 6, 1973

Bryant has been here almost every day bringing apple juice or fried chicken, which seems to be about the only thing I can keep down. Today he helped me catch Anastasia, the Suffolk ewe, and I cleaned and disinfected her foot. We managed then to get her into the VW van, and I drove her all the way to Half Moon Bay to Doc Dehner, who gave her a shot because of her runny nose and the sore on her mouth. She was pretty good, for a wild thing, but was glad to get home.

I had coffee with the new next-door neighbors, the Blacks, and we exchanged recipes, wood and jam.

San Pedro, California, March 11, 1973

Audrey has written to me and told me of the ordeal you have gone through re your daughter, Anna. My oldest sister's son vanished from home (in Tennessee) about three years ago and nothing ever was fully understood or brought to light re his disappearance. It was thought at one time (that) his father had taken him away. (His father killed my parents in 1954.) The FBI and all concerned authorities feel that he (my nephew) either "dropped out" or is dead.

Mikie, although I live pretty far from you, I'd be glad to help you in any way I can during this distressing time and after too.

You have come to mind many times since we said goodbye in high school. I remember ...you did a write-up about me once for a paper when I was "Miss Tennessee College Queen."

I'm 37 now (going on 10 in my mind--have much more maturing to do.) My once-brown hair is blondish and--would you believe?--all my pimples are gone! Now I'm working to adjust to the wrinkles.

My girls are ages 11 and 13 and named Carrie and Julie after the parts I played in "Carousel". Years ago I worked with Martha Raye in "Hello Dolly" (stage). Now I am doing a lot of creative writing, mostly for fun.

You are not forgotten in my prayers.
Fondly, Anita Barker (Congelliere)

March 18, 1973

Today we dedicated the Golden Goatway Bridge at Gene and Bryant's, a small footbridge built by Joe and the boys over one of the deep fissures in the cliffs at the beach near Tunitas Canyon. The goats loved it and ran right across and started looking for grass to eat. There was a full moon.

March 20, 1973, Tuesday

I threw the I Ching and the message was Deliverance, with no changing lines. As I was reading in the book, a male Anna's hummingbird, brilliantly colored, soared and dipped in the air outside and Moon and the other horses stood very still and watched. I walked down Purisima Creek Road to the wild place Anna called "God's garden" (actually, she asked me whose garden it was and I told her that) and picked two trillium, one purple, one white. At about 4:10 there was the most powerful moment of stillness. Perfect quiet everywhere. It has been eight weeks since she disappeared.

March 22, 1973

Science Fair for Eddie at Cunha.

March 23, 1973

American Conservatory Theater with Stan and the boys.

March 25, 1973

Tom and Marilyn Elias here.

Famagusta, Cyprus, March 27, 1973

I am deeply sorry for the disappearance of your daughter Anna. Did you search? Did you ask the proper authorities to help you? I am sure that you have done everything, before you came to the conclusion that she is lost.

As to us, we passed many difficulties as a whole family and only God knows how we managed to stay alive. I studied law and I am a practicing lawyer. Claire continues to teach in the gymnasium and she sends you her warm regards.

Nicos A. Angelides (Cyprus)

March 29, 1973

Food Club meeting. Work in San Francisco. Nonda, track meet.

Summertown, Tennessee, March 30, 1973

I woke up early this morning before the morning horns and went outside and heard the birds and stretched and you were all in my head as you are so much. I've gotten in an uptight place with myself cause I didn't write when I first got your letter. Every day I write letters in my head and think now I should have written before and maybe I could call and I love them and do they know that and on and on.

We all felt your losing Anna and send our love and compassion to you. We loved her too and having our own five know what you've felt. David is a big kid, nine in April. He sends his love to you boys and talks about how he'd like to see you again and play football. Christine is almost three, talking and goes to nursery school. Genevieve has just learned to walk. She's a groove, very round and blonde. And Roseanna is six months, crawling and smiling. Henry has left the farm for awhile. He wanted to live with his father in Vermont. Kaymarie had a baby boy Ezra and Ellen (Nancy) is pregnant again.

Marylouise, Joseph, Mary and William

April 10, 1973

Anastasia likes music and cheese crackers. She butts Saturn, the dog, if he gets too close to her. Just now I was playing the piano and she came to the window to listen and chew on a mouthful of grass, the way she always does.

April 11, 1973

The 3000th territorial war today over the farm. While Cherie Hooper and her collective Schoolhouse were still negotiating to rent the place, another couple is moving into the Queen Anne.

April 12, 1973

I packed away Anna's toys and clothes today. At first I cried, but then I kept finding little surprises and started thinking that I was taking care of things. She used to say "Take CARE of this." There was a little music box I gave her, something I got in Switzerland, I think, which played "Auf Wiederseh'n", that sentimental old saw: "Auf Wiederseh'n, Auf Wiederseh'n; we'll meet again, sweetheart. This lovely day has flown away; the time has come to part..." I could only listen to the first part of the song before I closed the top. I put everything away very carefully, in case she should ever need it. It was only three little boxes, but good stuff.

San Francisco, California, April 12, 1973
Your letter and news clipping re little Anna has been received. We remember with heavy heart when this tragedy happened and followed the story as it appeared on television, etc. We could do no more than advertise in the War Cry, our national Salvation Army magazine, for the child. An original photo would be needed--which would be returned to you. Let us know if you wish this done.

Cases like this are of course a matter for the authorities who have ways and means for an all-out search. We agree that it could be a case of kidnap.

We do hope and pray that one day soon something will come to light. As I sit writing and looking at your beautiful child I am weeping with you. We must not give up hope but keep faith and remember the Good Lord understands and does all things well.

We will keep in touch with you.

Sincerely, Pauline Eberhart (Lt. Colonel, The Salvation Army, Missing Persons Bureau)

April 16, 1973: Monday before Easter
Anna has been gone three months. I went out to put polyurethane on the bumper Joe made for my minibus and realized for the first time that Joe had made it out of the lovely clear redwood George had used for our bed. It started me thinking about having a respect for the variety of life forms. Almost as soon as I have a thought like that, something happens as if to test whether I really mean it. Gene arrived with a friend and a dog. Since I hate dogfights worse than anything, and since a visiting dog almost always means a fight

with Saturn, this was the test. Can I respect somebody's animal as well as the somebody? I don't know.

Test number two: Two different mothers beating on their children, seen while out shopping. There has to be a nonviolent form of discipline. Nonviolence has to be total and consistent, just as being non-threatening is the outward appearance of a peaceful self.

April 20, 1973, Western Good Friday

Our perceptions of time and space must be linked to our neural anatomy.

April 26, 1973

Visited the painter Galen Wolfe in his little house at the end of Frenchman's Creek Road. Canvases are everywhere, stacked against the walls, leaning on this, piled on that. He is a friend of Sue Small, and she paints with him.

April 27, 1973, Orthodox Good Friday

I called in sick at work today, afraid of the commute to San Francisco.

May 11, 1973

Sometimes I awake with so many questions it is hard to go on.

May 16, 1973

I can't sustain the not knowing. Although nothing has been found or proven, I think I can find peace if I just assume Anna died, somehow. I am trying to learn how to stay balanced, but it is difficult because I am alone so much and have so little energy. Many of my judgments seem insane to me in retrospect.

May 18, 1973

Anna's solution to summer flies was to wear a net onion bag over her head.

May 22, 1973

This felt like a normal day, the first for a long time. I gardened and practiced the piano.

May 25, 1973

Fulfillment of a lifelong ambition: I played piano with an orchestra. It was more than 150 high school, junior high and elementary music students from the Coastside. Tuning alone took half an hour.

May 30, 1973

I became ill and then violently nauseated. Despairing.

May 31, 1973

Asya, who was here the morning Anna disappeared, stopped by for a visit. He said he polished his brass bed for six hours and then his wife wouldn't let him sleep in it. "She kicks me out. I toss and turn."

June 3, 1973

A spider crawled out of this diary when I picked it up. Suzanne's family wants her to move away from here. It's true; it's no longer a very happy place.

June 4, 1973

Another spider crawled out of the book.

June 7, 1973

No spiders this time. Joe dreamed that Anna came back. She had a front tooth missing and had been taken by a mother who needed "another daughter". At first, he said, she couldn't figure out how to get home, but finally just started walking. Arlene called and said she dreamed of Anna wearing a long white nightgown, her hair pulled back, smiling as though she knew something and giving Arlene the feeling that she was going to telephone me and say she was all right. They want to give me hope. They want to have hope themselves.

June 8, 1973

My thirty-seventh birthday. My birthdays aren't sforzando any more, but rather crescendo-decrescendo.

San Francisco, California, June 25, 1973

The enclosed letter is self-explanatory. No doubt by now you have received a copy of the War Cry in which Anna's ad appears. How we do hope and pray for some word of the child. One of the photos is enclosed. The other will be returned to you later.

Sincerely, Pauline Eberhart (Lt. Colonel, The Salvation Army, Missing Persons Bureau)

CHAPTER ELEVEN

July 6, 1973

Joe said today he doesn't think we'll ever find her if she went into the creek. The big holes that were there during the storm are all silted up. *(However, see a subsequent geological report regarding Purisima Creek and silting in Chapter 13.)*

July 8, 1973

Carlos Castaneda, A Separate Reality: "Many men of knowledge do that--one day they may simply disappear....they choose to die because it doesn't matter to them."

July 11, 1973

I dreamed of Anna last night: That Joe called me and she was snuggled in bed with him. I asked her where she'd been (she was wearing a print blouse and a blue denim jumper) and she said "I don't know." I asked her if there was anyone there with her and she said, "Yes, Emily."

July 18, 1973

I think I was completely happy up until the time I was five. My parents were young, sunny, always doing things. I was free--I roamed the neighborhood. I had friends, I liked Miss Ella, my kindergarten teacher, I passed through things like a tornado with awe and excitement because I felt safe. The fact that I can remember quite a lot about the year I was five, even after an entire lifetime, is something of a comfort to me. Maybe she will remember us.

Dick has been checking on investigators, but the three he called have had their telephones disconnected.

July 19, 1973

I was thinking about what a passionate person she was. When she had been wronged (usually by some child who didn't want to play with her), she would run inside, her face all contorted and dark, in a breath-holding rage. She couldn't even cry until she had been hugged.

July 20, 1973

I found Nonda looking at her picture and crying.

July 27, 1973

   I remember a whimsical thing she made me from the bottom part of a flower pot with a cork stuck in it. Suzanne's brother helped her clean it and cut off the cork.

July 28, 1973

   The Explorer Scouts were here with their long hair, their changing voices and shovels. If she were in or near the creek and if she were going to let anybody find her, it might be these Scouts. They make me think of the Children's Crusade.

   Red, one of the horse owners, told Joe that he and the other horse people have been riding the trails and searching the hills and along the creek ever since Anna disappeared. She always liked his horse, Moon.

August 3, 1973

   The Sheriff's office called today with the results of an analysis of some bones the Scouts found. They are definitely animal bones, they said.

August 7, 1973

   Today Joe took a correlated report of search activities we got together to Captain Herbert Elvander at the San Mateo County Sheriff's Office and Captain Elvander said he'd put more energy into the investigation.

   Here is the report:

DETAILS OF SEARCH EFFORTS AND ANALYSIS OF MISAPPREHENSIONS WITH REGARD TO THE DISAPPEARANCE OF ANNA CHRISTIAN WATERS

   On January 16, 1973, five-year-old Anna Christian Waters, daughter of Mr. and Mrs. Joseph Ford, disappeared form her home at the Pimentel Ranch south of Half Moon Bay in San Mateo County, California. Despite a search involving several hundred people and continuing as of this date, August, 1973, no other fact is known by the family regarding her disappearance except that she did disappear.

   Because of the emotional reaction to the loss of a child, because of misleading newspaper reports, and because there have been many private and public search efforts without a correlation in order to rule out certain geographical areas, a number of misunderstandings have arisen regarding the case.

Chief among these are:

1. That footprints of the child were found beside Purisima Creek. Anna's mother initially stated that she thought she saw small footprints leading to the creek. Upon checking with neighbors, it was found that there were two sets of prints, one small, one large, and these were ascertained to have been the prints of a neighbor wearing size 4 boots of the same type and size as the oversized ones worn by the child, and those of a carpenter, who with the neighbor had run along the southern side of the Ford yard and the creek bank beside the mill house as soon as the child went missing.

2. That dogs tracked the child to the creek. One bloodhound was released near the creek about 17 hours after Anna's disappearance. A member of the Sheriff's Canine Unit told the family that they were lucky to get conclusive tracing with bloodhounds under ideal conditions with scents only two hours old. The ground was wet and had been walked over by many searchers by the time the dog was brought in. The owner of the dog nonetheless felt that the dog had gotten a scent. Curiously, the dog doubled back (upstream) before quitting. The path the dog used was one often used by children and animals at the farm. The tracking, of course, could not be regarded as conclusive in any sense.

3. That Anna's pet dog ran back and forth between the house and creek after her disappearance. This adolescent dog, the pet of the child's brother, was sitting calmly on the porch when first seen after the child was discovered missing. He was not a reliable barker or watch dog and only went to the creek when following the family or searchers.

4. That Anna had a pet rooster which had been killed that morning and which she may have tried to find at the creek. There was a fear, but no evidence, that she may have been curious about the rooster which had attacked her and other children and which that morning had been killed and thrown into the creek by a blacksmith whom it flogged. The remains of the rooster were found slightly downstream. This story was taken by the press and exaggerated, causing great distress to the blacksmith and to the family. The rooster was not a pet and was of only incidental interest to the child.

5. That a sock (or other item of clothing) was found which belonged to Anna. Five socks were found, one of them upstream, but none was identifiable as belonging to the child. Children frequently waded in the creek, as often as not taking off their shoes and socks and forgetting them. In addition to the socks, carcasses of cows, deer, small animals and fish were found. Bones found by Explorer Scouts July 28 were analyzed by pathologists and were found to be animal bones.

The report and spread of rumors regarding recovery of clothing, etc., has been grievous to the family and has added to the public impression that the child did drown when there has been no indication that this was so. Because the public opinion is that the child went into the creek, those who might have noticed had she appeared elsewhere were not watching for her.

6. That the dirt road adjoining Purisima Creek Road was impassable January 16, disallowing the possibility of kidnapping using an access to the town of Half Moon Bay which is not visible from the Pimentel Ranch. According to the post woman, Bud Machado, who drove over the road that day to deliver the mail, the road was passable, though narrowed by slides.

7. There is an inference felt by the family and neighbors that Purisima Canyon is "wild", with an indication that people living in such a "primitive area" might expect natural tragedies. The Half Moon Bay weekly newspaper frequently refers to the "wild" canyon area and did so in stories dealing with Anna's disappearance. There are 16 residences on the approximately 1 1/2 miles of Purisima Creek Road; the land between and beyond the residences is fenced pasture.

The Pimentel Ranch, purchased in 1972 and renamed "Rancho Canada Verde" by Lindsay M. Mickels, a Menlo Park attorney, contains three rental houses, one of which was temporarily unoccupied Jan. 16, a barn and meadows used for boarding horses, and several old sheds and buildings. About 3/4 mile up a Jeep trail is a hunter's cabin formerly used by the Bald Mountain Sportsman's Club and presently being used by the Sierra Club.

A casual count of cars over the paved portion of Purisima Creek Road any weekend may approach 200.

Purisima Creek is normally a mild, meandering creek with a few deep pools. In normal times it has been possible to wade almost the entire four-mile length of the creek. The extraordinary floods in January, 1973, were attributed by knowledgable residents to the destruction of the watershed by logging southeast of the creek which continued through winter of 1972. There were public debates of riparians with the logging company in the past regarding the disturbance of the local ecology, resulting in silting and pollution of the creek and presenting the possibility of flooding during heavy rains.

Therefore, though the creek may have been wild in January because of the effects of logging, the climate of the canyon, bordered by Skyline Boulevard, two meadow ridges and the Coast Highway, can hardly be said to be wild. We feel that an inference that we should not be surprised at a child's disappearing in the "wilds" is ignorant, personally prejudicial, and irresponsible.

8. It has been generally believed that neighbors were questioned as to their observations in an attempt to form an investigation into possibilities other than drowning. However, on July 30, the family asked all the neighbors of the 16 houses whether they had been questioned by officials or investigators with regard to Anna's disappearance. None had ever been questioned. Although two neighbors had noted somewhat unusual phenomena at the time, questioning at this point--six months after the fact--is of doubtful value.

9. That the child's body washed out to sea. Because of dams, log jams and barbed wire fencing across the creek, it was the informed opinion of searchers that this could not be true even under flood conditions. It is unlikely that the child's floppy vinyl or rubber boots would not have come off and been found somewhere. A professional diver and second-generation commercial fisherman, John Koepf (who had lived at the ranch until shortly before Jan. 16), said that he could not see how a 50-pound child could cross the many barriers if they stopped even small fish, but that if by the wildest chance this had happened, the body would have washed up on southern local beaches shortly because of tides and currents.

In the four or five drownings off the beaches since then, the bodies have been recovered within three days because of this tide factor. Nonetheless, the family on July 30 questioned fishermen below the Iacopi Ranch, where Purisima Creek flows into the ocean, whether they had seen any signs. They had not, and they had worked at that spot daily since before January. The beaches have been scanned since January and have revealed nothing. There are no unused beaches on this section of the coast. A radio station reportedly repeated the rumor that the child's body had been found at sea, causing great grief to the family.

PART II: DETAILS OF PRIVATE AND PUBLIC SEARCHES AS KNOWN TO THE FAMILY

January 16, 1973: 2 P.M., Anna last definitely seen by parents in the house. Between 2:15 and 2:20, the mother, not having heard the child's voice in the south yard for several minutes, went to look for her. When she did not answer, the mother became alarmed and began to search southward, in the direction of a chicken coop. Mrs. White and Mr. Barrick, who had been visiting at the house, searched around the millhouse near the bridge (east.) When the mother, doubling back, saw footprints there, she mistook them for those of the child, and this misapprehension was not clarified for two days (Mrs. White remarked that she and Anna had jokingly exchanged boots once.)

Although in retrospect the family thinks the child may have gone (north) to check the mailbox--she had just seen Mrs. White reading her previous day's mail--no one looked in this direction for some time. The Sheriff's office was called and an officer arrived at about 3 P.M., drove across the bridge and put on his siren. Mr. Barrick walked the jeep trail toward the hunter's cabin and others of the family looked in and around the three houses, along the creek banks, east on Purisima Creek Road about an eighth of a mile, and west for about a quarter mile. A neighbor, hearing the siren, reported that she had heard crashing in the brush where she was feeding animals about a quarter mile east on Purisima, and went back to look, followed by other volunteers. Divers, helicopter, searchers on foot and horseback from the sheriff's office continued to search the area until dusk. A car patrolled the road from the coast highway to the ranch all night. Telephones were out of order because of the storms, off and on for the next few days.

January 17: Morning, Ford and four friends drove to the ocean and checked the beaches. Bloodhound released for tracking at ranch. Youth camp volunteers, forestry service, family, friends and other volunteers searched the creek, the woods, hillside and environs, on foot and on horseback, south and west of the ranch and west in and along the creek to the Verde Road bridge, as well as all the buildings of the ranch, until dusk. Paul Borman, owner of Borman Kennels, overlooking the ranch, checked the creek with his dogs upstream on this day and the two days following.

January 18: Volunteer divers connected with the San Mateo sheriff's office searched the creek. Volunteer trail walkers searched the woods and northeast of the ranch.

January 19: Dr. George Stewart, a friend attending the family, and Joe Ford and the dog search the creek in wetsuits and were of the opinion that a body could not have gotten more than 100 yards downstream, due to debris and jam-ups.

January 20: Four sheriff's reserve divers search the creek. At this point, Sgt. Robert Lauffer said "I'm 90 per cent sure we didn't miss her, if she's in the creek." (Quoted in Half Moon Bay Review article.) Further official searches were postponed until the water level dropped.

January 21: John and Ernie Koepf, professional divers, and Ford in wetsuit search the creek; family, volunteers and dog search banks. Ford at this time found the carcass of the much-publicized rooster about a half mile downstream from the ranch.

January 22: The Fords retrace the dirt road leading to Higgins Canyon Road and establish that it would have been possible for a person to drive from Half Moon Bay and to observe the ranch from a number of spots without being seen. It was also possible to walk between the trees and the flooded creek bank all the way to the Pimentel Ranch without being seen.

January 23: Ford, a friend and the dog search the creek in wetsuits from a quarter mile northeast of the ranch, down to the ocean. Several volunteers from the sheriff's department, on their own time, also search the creek and banks.

January 24: Ford and three other friends complete to their satisfaction a search of debris, banks, log jams, etc., pulling out all but the largest log jams. At no point was any trace or sign of Anna found.

January 26: Sgt. Maguire and his superior come to look at the creek, ranch and environs.

February 5: Ford goes over the creek again with the dog, concentrating on a mile north to a mile south of the ranch.

February 7: Bank at the Machado ranch checked because of reports of a piece of clothing which proved to be a piece of plastic which searchers had thrown on the bank.

March 20: Mother searched along road northeast with the dog.

May: Joe Ford and Nonda Trimis search the length of the creek with the water at a low level. No trace or sign of Anna was found anywhere.

During this entire time, there were ongoing searches by neighbors and friends on foot and on horseback while riding, walking and camping in the area. There have been numerous incidences of independent searching in the woods, hills, and stream banks.

July 28: Joe Ford, Nonda Trimis, and two sheriff's deputies with Explorer Scouts and dog again search the creek, now at an extremely low level, cutting back brush and digging into silted areas, finding no trace. Some bones taken back to San Mateo for analysis prove to be animal bones, no surprise to Ford, who was convinced that he had missed nothing.

The barns and houses have been checked by Ford at least four times, and by other individuals as well, and were last checked within and without on July 26. Bill Pimentel, who homesteaded the ranch, volunteered very early in the search that there were no wells or pits on the property. Household water was taken from streams and from the creek.

PART III: CONCLUSIONS

Anna Christian Waters was born Sept. 25, 1967, at 4:44 P.M. at University of California-Moffitt Hospital in San Francisco. Her mother, Michaele, and father, Dr. George Waters, were divorced in the summer of 1969 on grounds and under circumstances which are a matter of court record in San Francisco. Anna continued to live with her mother and half-brothers until summer, 1971, when they and a family friend, Joseph Ford, took a camper trip around the country for six months, visiting relatives and having school lessons at various cities and sites.

In November, 1971, they came to live south of Half Moon Bay, on Purisima Creek Road. In 1972 Ford and Mrs. Waters were married and Anna began kindergarten at Alvin Hatch Elementary School. Her mother was a teacher's aide in the kindergarten class. Ford is a carpenter employed out of Redwood City Local 1401. Nonda and Edward Trimis, Anna's half-brothers, attend Half Moon Bay High School and Cunha Elementary School, respectively.

When last seen, Anna was wearing oversized (Size 4) black rubber or vinyl boots, blue jeans with a leather belt, a short-sleeved tee shirt with narrow blue and white pin stripes, and a ponytail holder. She removed her coat before leaving the house the afternoon she disappeared. She had short, curly sun-bleached blonde hair, a faint white mark discernable on a front tooth, and a small mole over the right cheekbone. She had a very small vaccination scar on the arm. In October, 1972, she was 44 1/2 inches tall and weighed about 45 pounds. Her height in January was about 45 to 45 1/2 inches, and her weight had probably increased a pound or two. She had no cavities or fillings in her teeth, and no missing teeth. Her footprint at birth is on file at U.C.-Moffit Hospital in San Francisco. The mother has a plaster cast of her handprint which was made at kindergarten.

Anna was very friendly to everyone and very independent and intelligent. She was never known to go to the creek or out of sight of the family house unaccompanied or without permission, except to the neighbors' yards or to the mailbox. Her brother's dog at the time of her disappearance did not consistently bark at strangers or always follow the children. At this time, the "regular" farm watchdogs had been gone for only about a week, since their owners, the Koepfs, had moved to Montara.

Some notes on Anna's father: He is driving a gray 1970 Volkswagen with the license number 653 ARH. Weekdays he works from 8 A.M. to 12 at the Mission Health Clinic, then from 1 to 3:30 at Presbyterian Hospital, Sacramento and Webster Streets, then 4 to 8 P.M. at Kaiser Hospital in Oakland, 580 Howe Street, off MacArthur Boulevard. He seems to have two hotel rooms, one on Geary Street, one on Polk, around the corner. He doesn't park in a garage.

August 9, 1973
Joe and Nonda dream of Anna all the time, but I must be repressing my dreams.

The Sea Ranch, California, August, 1973

Jai sita Ram. Hearing the news of disappearance of your beloved daughter, I feel sorry and pray god to give you all courage to face her separation. A person sees a beautiful girl in a solitary place, talks to her and finds her very friendly. Takes her to Mexico or south. Not due to enmity with you but due to a desire to have a child. Several people searched the creek and there is no trace of her and a five-year-old girl can't run away by herself. There are pretty good chances of being taken away by some crazy person. You tried your best to trace her out, now leave the matter in the hands of God, who gave her birth and will take care of her.

What more can you do except to pray God for her welfare.

Wish you all happy, Baba Hari Dass

Los Angeles, California, August 10, 1973

Sri Daya Mata received your letter and asked that you be sent the following message as she is away from the Mother Center at this time:

"Dear One, my heart went our to you when I read of the tragic disappearance of your little daughter Anna. Know for certain that I am deeply praying for her as I am for you and your wife. It is difficult to understand with the intellect why a just and loving God permits such tragedies to occur, but we must gain comfort in the realization that He is the beloved Father who has watched over all of His children from the time he created them. As Anna was yours to know and love in this life, so has that spark of divinity which is her soul belonged to God eternally. Continue to pray for her, sending your love, and she will receive it. Through the power of such love, you will be drawn together again, whether it be in this life or another.

I only wish it were within my power to give you some words of comfort and reassurance, but words are so inadequate to express what is within the heart and soul. I pray God may help you to find peace within and may guide you to inner knowledge He wishes you to receive about your dear little one. May the Divine hold you and your family ever in His love."

In divine friendship, Sr. Janaki

Confidential Secretary to Sri Daya Mata, Self-Realization Fellowship

August 10, 1973

It seemed like an act of will to recall last night's dream. My friends held a party and when the lights went on, there was Anna, standing on a stage in the room. I cried and hugged her. George had taken her away and put her in a small school. She looked just the same.

Jung, in Man and His Symbols, says "I have always insisted on the importance of sticking to the context of a particular dream and excluding all theoretical assumptions about dreams in general--except for the hypothesis that dreams in some way make sense.

Yesterday I talked for a long time with my neighbor Nancy Thurston. She said her husband and Bud, the mail woman, had walked Purisima Creek many times. She said it is obstructed from the ocean, not like San Gregorio Creek, which runs directly to the Pacific, and that they decided Anna had not gone into the creek.

Dharmsala, India, August 15, 1973

If I had wisdom I'd come back and help others with the struggle that is life, but I don't...I just made it into (the kindergarten) of Thubten Zopa Rinpoche (a 24-year-old very precious Tulku incarnated this lifetime across the border in Nepal) this lifetime, and who knows how many lifetimes it will take to develop wisdom.

I would like, if possible, to see a copy of the magazine you put out (The House Organ, begun in July, 1973.) Please, if it is no hassle? If we all didn't "know" so much, in fact, didn't know anything, we'd be so much more open to experience things as they really are. But it's a lot of hard work to undo all the conditioning, to learn not to know and keep it that way, flowing with the stream. What an incredible lesson it all is, how much pain and suffering, conditioned and habituated not to remember, how many times do we have to repeat it until we learn that it is mere creation of mind with nothing of substance to grasp.

Half Moon Bay has "nature romantics" (very funny in your letter). Dharmsala has "spiritual romantics" of the instant solution type, also "nature" ones and Himalaya instant enlightenment ones.
Usch

Thessaloniki, Greece, October 22, 1973

I can't tell you how touched I was by your letter of October 1st and the contribution in memory of little Anna. Sometimes a gift like that means every bit as much as a $1,000 contribution. It should somehow, because it is the giving and its spirit, much more than the amount, which has value both to the giver and the receiver. I'm not sure what we might do with it specifically, but we will at least start by planting a memorial tree and register her name in the (American Farm) School 's book of remembrance.

We think of you often and I know you are aware how much our prayers are with little Anna wherever she may be. Tad sends her love too.

Sincerely, Bruce M. Lansdale

October 31, 1973

Rachael came home with me yesterday while Phil and Lia were moving into their new house in Montara. It was a comfort to me, as though some of the things I loved in Anna were still embodied in that little frame. Rachael was still, awed, when we crossed the footbridge. She sensed or remembered some fear, I think. She said "What if the gander should pick me up and fly away?" She thought the ducks were wearing slippers.

Penny Brackney, the midwife friend of Michael S. up in the Gold country, "saw" that Anna was with the "son of a railroad man."

November 5, 1973

Joe seems to have slipped into desperation. I don't know what is happening to me. Sometimes I feel mystically transcendental, detached. Sometimes I feel too weary to continue. It seems as if there are no answers available to us, and that people want to forget that a child is missing and has not been accounted for.

November 11, 1973

Monday, the day before she disappeared, we went to school together. I helped her build a little wagon which she brought home the next day. The bus was late, and while we were waiting for it, she stepped on her teacher's feet. Ruth, the kindergarten teacher, thought she was being "testy", as she said, but I knew she was trying to dance with her.

The children in the kindergarten class were so disturbed that Ruth had to call in a therapist. "Will Anna grow up?" they asked. "If she died, she'll never get to grow up. I want to grow up," the children said. "Anna will grow up," Ruth told them. "If she doesn't get to grow up here, she'll grow up in heaven."

Round-faced, with dimples and curly blonde hair, Ruth may have looked something like Anna herself when she was a child. Her eyes are bright with intelligence and playfulness, and her lips curl up at the corners even when she is serious, as she was when she came to see me and brought a kind of autobiography Anna had made at school, with the names of her brothers and parents and pets. The aides asked the children to answer questions and wrote their answers. One of the questions was whether the child were happy or sad most of the time. Anna said that she was happy most of the time. "And you might think that all the children would answer that way," Ruth said, "but they didn't."

It was Ruth who told me about the power of boredom: Leave a child alone for two weeks, three, let her get really bored, and then you will see what boredom produces," she said. "She will build a tree house, paint pictures, make sculptures. Some parents try to schedule every hour for their children, and then they wonder why they are passive and uncreative."

Ruth invented the perfect good clean fun for the kindergarten class: A tub full of cornstarch dissolved in water. "You can do all sorts of things with it, and when it dries, it brushes right off," she said.

Things have changed so. Many of our friends and acquaintances seem to have withdrawn and we are surrounded by near-strangers. There have been many incidences of kindness, but also of amazing callousness. One woman was talking about cases she had heard of involving molestation of children. "Oh, I hope Anna went into the creek," she said. How could she say such a thing?

November 14, 1973

Two days ago in an awful storm, a 60-foot-tall tree was uprooted and crashed onto the footbridge, breaking the railing but resting on limbs on the bank opposite it before actually hitting the bridge itself. There was an earthquake that morning too. Where is she? Not knowing, every muddy bank, every crumbling board, every fallen tree makes me think of her and grieve. I don't want to associate her with negative things. Will I ever get over feeling that it is a shameful thing she managed to get away? Was there any way I could have held on to her?

We found this old duplicating machine in one of the barns and it became a big production, trying to make it work. We took it to A.B. Dick, whose employees were curious about it because it was so old, and they got it working and gave us stencils and fluid. We started joking about a publishing company called Thomas Paine Ditto Works, and then we started putting out a little magazine which we called the House Organ (of T.P. Ditto Works.) In the first issue, we had the log of the bus trip, or part of it, together with some of Anna's drawings, which raised some false hopes from people who glanced at it without reading the date; they thought somehow she had returned and nobody had told them about it.

The boys drew cartoons and wrote essays for the magazine, and we made a point of saying that nothing was copyrighted. Mother Earth News, missing the point, picked up one of the stories and reproduced it with a copyright notice.

For my stories, I chose a pseudonym with an eye to my Role in Life (I cannot write those words without a kind of inner twist), as in "What do you want to be when you grow up?" The answer to the question was the name Talking Bridge. A kind of translator of one kind or another.

Last night the Lutheran Church asked me to play the organ. I thought about how Anna used to play the piano for long periods of time, and how she liked her record player and the Beatles records, "Strawberry Fields Forever" and "Here Comes the Sun." I played "Amazing Grace" for the Lutherans. But Anna was my Amazing Grace.

November 23, 1973

Thanksgiving. I was thinking about the people who logged Hatch Woods, which certainly contributed to the flooding and silting of the creek. I want somebody to blame.

Santa Cruz, California, Dec. 6, 1973
Michelle and Anna were both in (Ruth's) class. Thank you so much for your letter. I didn't know your last name. Michelle was full of fun and free. She had no fears She was on her way home in sight of the house.

Affectionately, Michelle's family
(Parents of Anna's kindergarten classmate who was found dead.)

December 16, 1973

Yesterday I finished running off copies of Eleusis on the resurrected ditto machine. These are all poems of Demeter and Persephone. The lost daughter. Joe treated all the sheep for foot fungus and they're outside grazing peacefully. They'll even let the chickens hop on their backs to pick off bits of hay. I found a hidden nest in the chicken coop with 16 eggs in it, and the jonquils have big buds, so they'll be open for Christmas.

MORNING: THAT OF GOD IN EVERY THING

We missed the services yesterday;
the exigencies of fencing, searching
and bridge-mending
fixed us in space,
so I held services
with the creatures.
My second son sang his music
As I sat near the birds;
the crippled one stood
facing the sun, stretching out
his trembling leg,
caught in the moment.
The dog sat beside me,
resting his chin on my hair,
his eyes distant.
The sun reflected off wet grasses all around
and for a minute the ewe stood
and sniffed the air.
What was this among us?

December 18, 1973

It is sad and unfestive to be preparing for Christmas without Anna. We put the Christmas tree in her cradle.

December 19, 1973

How amazing to think that only a year ago our pastoral Purisima life was still intact. Suzanne and Bill were here, and Peggy with John and Shawn, Gina and Daisy. I was distributing the Farmers' Feed Cookbook Suzanne and I got together. She and I went to Macy's to get records for the record player I was getting Anna for Christmas. Anna was making Christmas cards with Nonda and me.

(Christmas card drawn by Anna in 1972)

One of her favorite sayings was "It can't die; it's made of plastic", which sounds curiously like something Suzanne might say.

Imagine: We plug the little Christmas tree lights in to see if they still work, and they do. "Careful! Don't step on them!" we warn Anna. She watches her feet.

She feels the bulbs. Her thumb and forefinger turn translucent, pink, holding the bulbs. "Don't burn yourself!"

"It's not hot." She wraps the strand of lights around her neck, holding the cord very carefully. "Look! Look at me!" Her curls are illuminated by the bulbs like that spun glass they used to call angel hair. "I'm a Christmas tree!"

And seeing that the bulbs are barely warm, we join in the game and wrap the lit strands around each arm, around her waist, back up to her head, a crown of lights. Her brother plucks the tin star from its tissue paper and places it atop her head and we all sing "Oh Christmas Tree, O Christmas Tree" while she squirms with pleasure.

It didn't really happen. It's a daydream to counter the nightmares about what could have happened to her. But it is exactly the sort of thing she, and we, might have done if we had thought of it.

CHAPTER TWELVE

January 16, 1974

It is a year today that she disappeared, and outside rain and gale force winds are raging, just as they were last year. The calla lily I rescued is just opening its pretty blossom today. One out-of-season plum clings to the tree outside.

Last night I dreamed I was working a weekend at the News-Sentinel and was talking to Gunby Rule (who is dead) and others who are presumably alive. I fell asleep in the dream and didn't wake until the next edition was done.

In the next part of the dream, I was drawing a diagram of Anna's face and head, showing neurocirculatory anatomy in blue and red, with the idea of recreating her. A mysterious voice behind me said "Of course it can be done" and went over the "circuits" in order to check and correct them. Those toward the front and top were all correct, but the mysterious presence corrected some at the base of the skull, covering up the blue lines I had drawn with a cross of red mystic tape (no pun intended.) At this point, Joe woke me up to say goodbye.

I put a sign on the front door and am sitting on Anna's little lavender rug, the one Father Hilarion at Himalayan Academy gave her when she was only a few days old.

At two o'clock exactly, Ruth, Anna's kindergarten teacher, called, remembering Anna, so sweet. She says she keeps a picture of Anna on the wall where she can look at it often. She thought this would be a hard day for me to get through and wanted me to know someone else was thinking of me. All the children, she said, always remember Anna as laughing and dancing. Anna's friend Kelly not long ago was doing something with music and said "You know, Anna would have loved that!" They were born the same day and year. Ruth is the only person who knows the right thing to say. I wonder how she has become so wise.

March 31, 1974

Today the boys and I put in Anna's garden, which we dug up at the farm and transported to our new house in Montara. There is the stump, the bergamot mint, chrysanthemums, all her little rocks. We added a hen-shaped flower pot and lovely canyon flowers: forget-me-not, alyssum, miner's lettuce and chamomile.

We have hung on at the farm as long as we could so we would be there if Anna reappeared. How will she find us now if she comes back? We tried to explain to the landlord. A new couple moved into the Queen Anne, Jim and Johnnie. Johnnie works at the Abalone Shop with John and Peggy, who have moved to Montara. I told Johnnie that we couldn't pay more rent; that we weren't working full time because we were looking for our daughter. "Yes," she said, "but what will you use for an excuse next time?"

Suzanne moved to New Mexico, away from the mildew and the memories and the crumbling bathroom walls. In lieu of air conditioning, she carried a water bottle with a spray nozzle. We watched her Volvo pull out, loaded with belongings, the door dented by one of Bill's miscalculations.

Whenever a place at Purisima became vacant, it seemed as if everyone in the world wanted it. In addition to the hunters' club, the motorcycle club, the horse people, the visitors showing friends where they used to live, there was a steady stream of people looking for a place to rent. The landlord's carpenters were there, making the coops and shacks into houses. They took over the mill where Joe kept his tools and said we had to put the tools somewhere else. The landlord hired our neighbor as the farm manager, in charge of the construction projects, and he said we needed to find another place to live.

We set out to find a place nobody wanted, and it appeared as a stucco house in Montara, fourteen miles north, which had been on the market for many months. We borrowed from friends and family to make the down payment. But how will she find us?

April 3, 1974

Yesterday Ed and I looked at the swollen and raging creek while searching for the grossly pregnant Patchouli (by Lionel? He visited us briefly not long ago). Little Dana was telling me at her piano lesson yesterday that the creek was up to her dad's knee. It must be as clean and round on the bottom now as a rubber tire. There is sand on the banks where it has gone down. The treehouse where we were married is like an island in the middle of the creek, with no way to approach it. The bridge has been undermined and they have hung a sign on a rope barring entrance.

June 4, 1974

I had such a vivid dream of Anna last night. She was playing with some other children. I opened a whitish-blue door from the bottom up, and there she was. She said "Mommy, did you fire me by accident?" I laughed that she had learned the word "fire" and reassured her that I had not fired her.

July 3, 1974

I sat up and read Edgar Cayce's Story of Karma, the whole big book, last night, and was left with a funny feeling about him. So far I haven't had any experience of a psychic, first-hand or in books, that I thought was completely believable. Their stories seem to be more or less consistent "dream creations" of the person who produces then, because he or she focuses on the images which seem important to him or her.

August 5, 1974

I continue to be sad and to have terrifying thoughts about Anna. What can I do now more than I could then? The dark side.

So I thought I'd try to recreate a memory of her in her daisy outfit. I made it for the school Halloween party, the Halloween after her fifth birthday, out of stuff from Sue and Cliff Small's barn. It had some sort of green dress-thing for a stalk, with big wire-rimmed satin leaves at the shoulder. Actually, she wanted to be a rabbit for Halloween, but I didn't have anything to make a rabbit suit out of. The hat was the petals and all. She really liked it. Becky's mother came to give her a ride to the school party. Becky wore a Hawaiian outfit, grass skirt and lei. Becky's mother raved about Anna's costume. I can see Anna getting into the car, trying to keep her petals in place. Little-girl excitement.

She wore the costume again in the melodrama our food club put on, "The Saga of Spanishtown Sue." She was the garden.

August 11, 1974

At Nonda's suggestion, I just wrote a letter to George. I felt funny about doing it, but Nonda said "they should WANT to help."

I am reading Edgar Cayce's book, The Sleeping Prophet. He tells of a spider dream.

"In this dream, there is seen the symbolic conditions of these forces as are being enacted in the life of this body. And, as is seen, both the spider and the character of same are as warnings to the body as respecting the relations of others who would in this underhanded manner take away from the body those surroundings of the home...that are in the manner of being taken...unless such a stand is taken...For, as is seen, the conditions are of the nature emblematically shown by the relations of this body with this other body (the woman); that its relations at first meant only the casual conditions that might be turned to an account of good, in a social and financial manner; yet, as has been seen, there has come the constant drain on the entity, not only in the pocket, but in the affections of the heart, and now such threaten the very foundations of the home; and, as seen, threaten to separate the body from the home and its surroundings; and unless the entity attacks this condition, cutting same out of the mind, the body, the relations, the conditions, there will come that condition as seen...Beware! Beware!"

I have looked for some interpretation of the spider nightmare Anna had a day or two before she disappeared, since she wasn't really afraid of spiders.

According to Cayce, virtually everything is dreamed before it happens.

September 10, 1974

Rachael is staying with us while Josh has his tonsils out. She went with me to Purisima for Dana's piano lesson. When we stopped for an ice cream cone, she told me she had a sort of funny dream "a week ago." "A Mommy was in a hurry," she said. "She tried to get the little girl to hurry, and she dropped her doll." Rachael said she didn't know who the people were. On the way home, she fell asleep and now is having a nap in Nonda's bed as I write this.

September 21, 1974, 7 A.M.

I just had one of those detailed "movies" I sometimes get as I am waking up. George goes up a flight of stairs with groceries. There is an elevator, but he walks three or four flights of stairs. He is tired/wired, flaming. He knocks on the door, once. His companion, Brody, answers. He takes the groceries. George sits down, takes off his shoes, goes to bed, starts to do a sort of shoulder-stand thing. Brody has instructed him to do this to relax. George's field is spotty, rare and wild, but Brody's is almost nonexistent. The "powers" he once claimed are gone. They do not know they are being observed. In the grocery bag are bread, cheese, a bottle of Pompeian olive oil, a bottle of brandy. Brody makes sandwiches. There is a big old television set which they often watch.

To the immediate right of the door is a desk. Here I am able to see a long, straight road. At first there are trees along the right, fields on the left. It is Bakersfield. Then we come to a house. There is tall shrubbery on the left, fields on the right. It is very flat and open. The shrubbery makes an "L" to the right of the house, but the rear is open. The roof has a line to it which Joe says is a gambrel roof. The house is white; the roof and shutters on the front are brown. Behind the hedge there seems to be a chain-link fence. The house is two stories tall and has a chimney. There is a woman with long dark hair cooking breakfast, scrambled eggs. The children are still asleep. Anna is here. Her hair has been dyed brown. The children do not go to school. They do not go outside often. The woman says they are foster children. She is a nurse. Pathetic, full of hopes. Believes George had a right to take Anna away. Innocent, really.

September 22, 1974

Looking at the photographs Asya took of Anna with the Park policeman's horse, so full of life and so typically full of wonder and daring. I remembered the time we went to the zoo and she tried to feed the elephant and he had her whole fist up his trunk.

(Anna in Golden Gate Park, circa 1970)

September 25, 1974

My retreat was peaceful, though not dramatically so. There were three kidnappings on the news, one in Cincinnati, two in San Jose, two little girls returned, one found dead, one other in San Jose missing for a long time…and still this strange equilibrium.

Today is Anna's seventh birthday. At 4:44, the hour she was born, I sat near her little garden. A bird came close and hopped around in the cypress tree. The ducks were quiet, as though they were listening. An apple fell off the tree and I ate it.

I felt peaceful...watched the reflections in the pool....tired after working hard all day. I felt that she was well and safe and free, but I can't know. Not yet. But this happy level where I meet with her is where we are one.

September 28, 1974

Last night I dreamed a continuation of the previous night's dream, with the same sort of setting, a stone wall, castle-like, a church? I told Anna I had dreamed she had a book called "Family Life", sort of a women's lib-type children's book, and she said "Yes, I do," and ran to get it from her suitcase and showed it to me. She seemed very grown up. She said "They wanted to get me lots of books, but I got just this one. I told them I had plenty of books at my home." These words made me happy that she remembered, and that she wouldn't be bribed with gifts.

She was still wearing that pink sweater. I started thinking "She's really here! We should call people and tell them!" I went to the phone to call Michael S., but there was no number except for his folks in Monterey, and Byron's number was no good because he was in Europe. Then I thought I would call my parents, but I don't remember doing it. The kind of funny thing is that "family life" is what the boys call their privates, as in "He kicked me in the Family Life!"

November 25, 1974

I completed the story I've been working on for so long, "Wide Open in Bakersfield", and sent it off--so difficult, so many facts and so much internal resistance. Just after I mailed it, I got a letter from Audrey Henry about my angel dream, a letter which would have caused me not to mail the article if I'd received it first.

The dream was this: Adrienne Arow, a high school classmate who sang at my senior piano recital and who died young, appeared to me in a dream as an angel with huge, multi-colored wings. I asked her if she still sang, and I was about to ask her if she knew where Anna was, but she turned (with a kind of wry smile, I think) and flew away, toward the light. My impression was that my question was completely beside the point--that her soaring flight was the most wonderful kind of song, and that I would have to be wiser in order to understand the answers to my questions.

Audrey's Jungian pastor interpreted the dream as a "direct message from God" that I was not to know in this lifetime what happened to Anna, and that she was in God's care.

January 6, 1975

Early in the morning I had another dream; Anna said she was at 2120 Georgian Place, Humboldt. Then I appeared in her nightmare, which had something to do with crying and the absence of me and a plane crash where she pointed to a mount of earth and said "right here". She then explained to me that I was in her nightmare and we hugged and I told her to call me on the telephone.

This morning, rain, cold, dreariness. These two years have taken their toll on me. Sometimes I sink into a despair so black that even tears don't come to relieve its cynicism. I want only to be left alone, to stare at the veil of this mystery until I am dead or insane.

January 16, 1975

I worked at Coastside Books today, doing inventory, etc. Felt very together and tidy and compulsively neat. When I got home, Ruth called. I looked at the calendar and saw that it is the 16th, two years since Anna disappeared. I had decided to have a normal day, and I did.

Ruth reiterated the class's reactions to and remembrances of Anna. I was again so touched...but I was conscious of mentally resisting the idea of her death and was relieved when Ruth said something about not knowing what had happened. Then I tried to think back to what I was doing about 2:30...the only thing special I remember is that I noticed Dianne's bathroom faucet dripping with the same tinkling melody I have heard on our faucets at the farm and here at the house (even with a new washer this week!)

April 30, 1975
      Today the last helicopter left Vietnam.

CHAPTER THIRTEEN

California Living, the magazine of the San Francisco Sunday Examiner and Chronicle, published my story about the search for Anna on April 20, 1975.

I wrote:

Saturday afternoon, driving south on Highway 5: The great irrigation canal cuts across the hazy valley and on either side of it emerald fields stand in stark contrast with the burnt yellow grass farther away. Joe and I are taking a leap of---not faith, but hope. We are driving to Bakersfield because I had a dream that our lost daughter was there.

In the dream, I saw her looking out the window of a white house with a brown gambrel roof and brown shutters. There was a hedge in front with a chain link fence behind it. The address was 2120 Gary, Bakersfield. We telephoned Yellow Cab in Bakersfield to see if there was a Gary street or avenue and learned that there was a Gary Place. Could it be that we will find the house with the brown roof?

Almost two years ago, our daughter, who was then five years old, disappeared from our home south of Half Moon Bay. Perhaps you read about it or saw the story on the television news. There was no follow-up. We did not learn, and do not know now what became of her. All we know is where we searched and what we tried to rule out.

The official San Mateo County Sheriff's office report, 73-0484, Missing Person, tells the bare facts.

"Missing five-year-old female. Date reported 1/16/73. Time reported 1500 hours. Time last seen 1415 hours. Probable destination unknown. Cause of absence: Lost. Hair, blonde, eyes, brown. Height, unknown (it had been 44 1/2 inches when measured two months before); weight forty pounds. Occupation, student.

"Statement of mother: She stated that her daughter in question was in the house between 1400 and 1415 hours and at that time removed her coat and went back in the yard to play. She stated that approximately fifteen minutes after her daughter had left, it was very quiet outside and she proceeded out the door to call her to the house. She stated that she called her a few times and she did not appear. She stated at this time the friends that were in her residence also exited from the house and attempted to locate Anna in the immediate area of the house.

"She stated that after they had checked the area around the house and the area of the creek, she panicked and called the Sheriff's office. This deputy arrived at approximately 1515 hours."

Even though it is Sunday, there is little traffic on Highway 5 going to Bakersfield. We proceed south at a steady fifty-five miles an hour, making small talk, shuffling maps. We are trying not to get our hopes up, not to feel foolish for following a dream...
.

. I have become a specialist in the field of lost children. I wonder what the figures are and how many children disappear and are not found each year? I have noted dozens of cases since my daughter disappeared.

I also have information on the unavailability of white Anglo-Saxon children for adoption. On the cloistering of the children of Krishna-followers in Texas. On the disappearance of Patricia Hearst. Television shows on kidnapping. Fiction: Silas Marner. Poetry: Little Girl Lost and Little Girl Found. Niobe. Job. Especially Job. Demeter and Persephone. Our literature and our mythology, even our scripture, are full of lost children.

We heard of one lost child whose parents initiated a prayer vigil and asked people of every faith to pray for the little boy's safety and return. He had been kidnapped, it resulted, and he was returned safely to his parents. At the suggestion of Anna's godparents, we asked for prayers, too...

We stop for gas at Gilroy. We are directed to a truck stop for breakfast.

In the shock and disbelief, a primitive reptilian consciousness takes over. Rule out the most immediate danger. We went first to the creek which flowed near our house, because it was winter deep and rushing. During the search it was walked in, dived in, flown over, dug in, sifted from its source to its outlet on the Pacific.

Four days after Anna disappeared, the local newspaper quoted sheriff's diver Sergeant Robert Lauffer: "I'm ninety per cent sure we didn't miss her, if she's in the creek.

"The greatest search in coastside history," the Half Moon Bay Review called it. Buses full of honor camp inmates joined deputies, frogmen, independent divers, horsemen, helicopter pilots, Explorer Scouts, friends, teachers, bus drivers, neighbors. Anna's disappearance seemed a personal loss to a lot of people.

Never at any point was any sign or trace of our daughter found in or near the creek. Some small footprints were found to be those of a searching neighbor who had jokingly exchanged boots with Anna the day before.

A champion bloodhound was brought in to the creek area after seventeen hours, but a member of the Sheriff's Canine Unit told us that they were lucky to get conclusive tracings under ideal conditions with scents only two hours old. The tracking was, of course, inconclusive after so much time, so man searchers' footprints, wet ground. Curiously, the dog doubled back, upstream, before quitting.

The telephone rang incessantly. It became harder and harder to say "No. Nothing."

Then we tried to rule out the surrounding countryside, because starvation and exposure are slower dangers than drowning. Actually, ground search had begun immediately, but now we concentrated on the countryside surrounding the farm. We searched every inch of the area by foot and on horseback, with dogs, binoculars, helicopter. Nothing. We did all this although Anna had never, in five years and four months, wandered off by herself or gone to the creek alone.

The last thing we tried to rule out was kidnapping. But by now a lot of time had passed. The area of pain was delineated and described, and no one wanted to approach it.

If Anna had died, then it was over. If she had been kidnapped, then it had only begun. People had made up their minds; they had achieved closure. She was beautiful, she was little, she was nowhere to be found. The pain found parallels in everyone. If they had children, they feared it could happen to them. If they had ever suffered a loss, the reminder was too much to endure.

It seemed that the more sensitive the individual concerned, the more complete was his closure on the subject. Everyone--except for us, the family, and a few close friends--had created an opinion of what had happened. The opinions were sometimes wildly contradictory and none could be checked out. But nobody wanted to reopen the subject.

No one had been questioned regarding unusual passersby or traffic. Now they couldn't remember. The sheriff's office said that there was a "probability" of abduction at this point. There was nothing they could do. "Where do we start?"

The kindness, even heroics, of the official and unofficial people involved in the search, had been extraordinary. They had given everything they could, and they could bear no more. What could we do?

We thought about contacting people with extrasensory perception. But we didn't know where to start. A friend wrote the pioneer researchers in ESP, the J.B. Rhines, and received an unencouraging answer...So we went back to the creek again. At least it was there and could be searched.

The first week, Joe explored the creek in a wet suit along with a dear doctor friend. Although there were professional divers at work, he wanted to be there, too. He wanted to know what to expect, and he was prepared to find Anna's body in daily progressing stages of decomposition. Every time he went into the creek it was an agony; every time he came out, having found nothing, we felt we had come closer to ruling out the creek as an answer to the mystery.

He found the remains of old Hulk, the rooster who had had his neck wrung and been tossed into the creek by a blacksmith the same day our daughter disappeared. He found little fish, flotsam and jetsam. He found socks, the result of summer wading and high winds whipping at clotheslines. He found the remains of two cows, a deer, mice.

"But water does funny things. Water and fire do funny things," said Detective Brendan Maguire, who was on the case now. Soft-eyed, tough-skinned with a brogue.

When Joe explored everything else, he went back and pulled apart the animal corpses so that he could look beneath them. He did it with his hands. He found nothing. The creek was purged for him. It became innocent again.

Other divers continued to pull the creek apart for weeks. Every log jam was gone over or removed, every drift probed, every pool searched until summer, when the creek depth was down to a few inches. Even then, we continued to walk the length of the creek, looking, ruling out.

Six months after Anna disappeared, Explorer Scouts found the cow bones and took them to the sheriff's pathologist for analysis. Could we have missed anything? Again, the agony, being reopened. The report after two weeks was definitive: animal bones...

Highway 5, south to Bakersfield. Now we are passing fields full of cotton, some of it harvested into bales, covered with plastic. I look at Joe, driving with an inscrutable expression, and remember a time when he was driving our school bus, the 35-foot 1947 Gillig, through cotton fields in Arkansas.

Joka--Anna named him that--was her real father as far as she was concerned, although she was told about her genetic ancestors and shown their photographs. When we lived in San Francisco, Joka would button her into his big army surplus coat and the two of them would drive around the city on his little Honda motorcycle. They looked like some strange kangaroo couple, one head dark and unruly with a big mustache, one little, blonde, curly, laughing and rolling its eyes.

She liked to drive past UC Hospital and look up to the fifteenth floor, where she was born. There was an earthquake while we were there, September, 1967, which rocked the beds in the maternity wing.

When we engineered the great bus trip, we drove the Gillig up the Parnassus hill and past UC once again. In all that expanse of bus, we had one driver (Joe), one cook/teacher (me), one navigator, twelve years old, one mechanic, nine and a half, and one passenger. This was our family. The passenger was Anna, and she bunked down in her own special carpeted cubicle built over the right rear wheel, next to the heater. We went everywhere, saw everything, had a wonderful time, and concluded the trip at the farm south of Half Moon Bay.

The next fall she started kindergarten. She loved the farm, the flowers, the horses. She adored school. I missed her, so I became a teacher's aide and went with her on Mondays. She loved her friends and was loved in return.

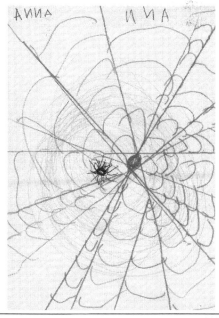

Two nights before she disappeared, she had a nightmare and was afraid. She came into our room and wanted to crawl into bed with us, where it was safe. We were glad to have her. "I dreamed a spider was chasing me."

The Talmud says "A dream that is not interpreted is a letter that is unread." After the fact, I looked everywhere for interpretations of spider dreams. Jung was equivocal, the occultists contradictory.

I wrote Hugh Lynn Cayce, son of Edgar Cayce, who was called "the sleeping prophet", (and he referred me to a psychic.) Then I found an interpretation of a spider dream by Cayce himself in the book, The Sleeping Prophet. The spider was interpreted as representing a woman who was about to steal the subject away from his family...

Bakersfield. We drive through the town, looking for gambrel roofs. We see one, two, a dozen. I never saw so many gambrel roofs before. Bakersfield is full of gambrel roofs. There are none, however, on Gary Place, and the street numbers go no lower than 2200.

We drive up and down Gary Place, looking at the faces of the children. One throws mud at our car. We drive up and down the cross streets. One house has sheep in the yard; another, cows. There are several poor-looking churches in the neighborhood, one made from a quonset hut. But there is no house here like the house in the dream.

We stop at a small grocery store for a drink and show Anna's photograph to the grocer. No, she has never seen her. She would be seven now. Would she look the same?

We drive down Gary Place once more. We stop, sit in the car, not knowing what to do. It is a long drive from the San Mateo coastside. A long drive here, and a long drive back...

I know she may be dead. I was ready to accept that. But there was never any indication that it was so. I feel that she is alive, in the body, and that she would get home if she knew how. To support this feeling is harder than closing down. It is as valid as any other conclusion, given what we know. What can we do that we have not done?

I review the dream that brought us to this town, 700 miles away from home. I think of the dozens of other dreams we and her brothers have had of Anna. Always she is well and doesn't know how to get home. I think of all the places we have looked for her, of the hundreds of people who were involved...

In the afternoon I drove for awhile and Joka slept. After the depression lifted, there was a moment of grim relief. We had checked out the dream and found nothing. That was that. We had absolutely ruled out the presence of a gambrel-roof house at 2120 Gary in Bakersfield in November of 1974. We had achieved closure on that matter.

But I didn't think it would last.

After the article about Anna's disappearance appeared in California Living, the (then) Sunday magazine of the San Francisco Examiner and Chronicle, Editor Harold I. Silverman and Managing Editor Jane Ciabattari screened letters and telephone calls and forwarded some to the family. Most of the letters had to do with psychics.

Oakland, California, April 20, 1975

I read your article about your missing daughter and found it very moving. I also experienced some other things that I hope will be of help to you. Immediately after putting down the paper I was struck with the letters P-U-N-M-A-T. I thought there must be a town of this name. I thought of the word Putnam. I also "heard" the word Elizabeth. I checked on my map and near Bakersfield there is a town called Tupman. Then I "felt" that if you went to a schoolyard and looked for your daughter Anna when school is in session or letting out you may find her there. I don't know what Elizabeth means. I felt it was the name of the woman who took your child.

Please believe my sincerity and concern. I hesitated to write this letter because I have never written anyone care of a newspaper, especially about a matter like this, but the messages seemed so clear and real that I had to write. I'm not a professional psychic, but I have had ESP and PSI experiences all my life. And I have gone through the Pecci-Hoffman therapy at the PSI institute in Oakland.

It just seemed very right-on to me.

Also I feel the woman who has taken Anna from you is gentle and not dangerous. She was just very lonely and wanted a child. And although she is not rich, she loves her very much and cares for her the best she can. I feel you approach finding Anna with an absence of retribution for the woman and let your love for Anna guide you. If you can have acceptance and understanding for the woman who took her from you, you will find her sooner. This may sound strange, but again it is what I feel.

I hope this information will help you find your daughter.
Sincerely, B.S

Orinda, California, April, 1975

I read your article today in the Chronicle--and I remember being moved by the original account of Anna's disappearance. You'll probably receive many letters like this, but just in case, I felt I had to write to you...I myself would not put a closure to the Bakersfield dream. Would it not be possible to discover which southwestern or southern states (to begin with) had a town called Bakersfield or a Gary Street without having to go there? By way of directories? And should there be such a small town in existence, mightn't it be possible to check the schools in the town? Second, or perhaps third grade teachers--sending photographs, asking whether there is a child named Anna or who remembers having been called Anna (for a child would tell people such a thing.)
(She offers various suggestions for the search, based on the dream mentioned in the article.) I would, at least, cover states that seemed to be applicable, with what various sensitives have said (especially with people of the caliber of Hari Dass Baba and Hugh Lynn feeling as they do about it.) ...The article in California Living will have changed the vibrations so tremendously so that with all these people reading the story now made aware, you really are "wide open in Bakersfield" in a much deeper way--and things are bound to happen. You may get so many suggestions that that form of prayer could be a protection, too, to help guide you correctly. Bless you and Anna and your family, and may God's love and power go with you in your search.
Sincerely, P.F.

Newark, California, April 22, 1975

Likely (Anna's mother) is aware that there is a Bakersfield in TX and Mo.
Sincerely, R.B.

San Francisco, California, April 22, 1975

On occasion I read the newspaper. Your story, "The Search for Anna Waters", moved me emotionally and spiritually. I pray you find your child. On my own with the help of Mrs. Costas of San Jose telephone service I called all the area codes. Here is a list of three other places. Bakersfield could also be the name of a person.
C.S.

Pacifica, California, April 26, 1975

Have you considered sending Anna's picture to county school offices throughout California? We've just learned they will respond and will ourselves be doing this shortly. Feel free to call if we can do more..
L.T.

April, 1975

I remember the beginning of the very sad thing when your child was lost. I never was able to find out if she was found until I read your article in California Living this Sunday.
A few weeks ago or possibly a month ago Merv Griffin had four or five people on his program who gave very good predictions. They all have a very good record. One was Carrol Richter (name may be spelled wrong). I see his horoscopes each day in the paper. There was one woman whose name I can't recall...who had predicted Nixon would resign. She also said the Queen would abdicate and her son would take her place. I also saw where that was confirmed....I have gone to Pearl Shannon on many occasions. I believe she is good.
Mrs. A. P.

TELEPHONE MESSAGES IN APRIL, 1975, IN RESPONSE TO CHRONICLE ARTICLE:

1. M. L., Burlingame: Did we circulate a photograph among teachers, district principals, superintendents, etc.? There's a 1974-75 directory listing all school principals in the state.

2. D. E., private investigator, San Francisco: Suggests psychic Peter Hurkos, whom they used to locate a crashed plane. Says he found it exactly, using a map. Says send a copy of the article with a piece of cloth from Anna's clothing.

      Telephoned Peter Hurkos. Requires that we be there in person (southern California) with all clothing of the child which hasn't been washed or dry-cleaned, photographs of the child and the yard, map of the area, a map of the United States, and a cashier's check for $5000. Peter Hurkos works five days and five nights straight through, must have advance notice, has a very high rate of success, but makes no guarantees. "He likes to work with police," his secretary said, "and you can bring them along if you like."

3. Pacifica woman: Her daughter was taken away from her home in Fresno by the father at age five, two years ago. Wondered if we had checked out Anna's father. Suggests the National Reuniting Center in Bellflower, California (a matching service with a $10 fee.) On April 29, 1975, sent check and application.

4. Mary S. dreamed that she had a call from Peninsula Hospital saying that the little girl who was lost had been found and that her name was Eva Sullivan. Mary asked them to check the name again and they said Eva Blackburn. Mary said she telephoned the hospital this morning, but no missing child had been brought there.

5. The National Reuniting Center called to give telephone numbers of three well-known psychics, all in southern California.

May 15, 1975
Tulare County Welfare Department
Re Donna, born May 15, 1964.

Mr. Fisher showed me your letter and since I have worked with Donna for the past three years, it was felt that I would be more able to answer your letter. I am very sorry to hear about your missing daughter and hope that you will be able to locate her soon. Also, I am sorry to tell you that our Donna cannot possibly be your missing daughter inasmuch as I have been Donna's worker since she was seven and before then, she's been in one foster home since she was three years of age. The foster parents had legal guardianship. She has been under the care of our agency since she was seven years of age and I have seen her on a regular basis since then. I have been with her quite closely, also, during the time you mentioned your daughter disappeared.

Marilyn O.
Adoption Worker

Kingston, Tennessee, June 30, 1975

Nannie (my maternal grandmother) *has been very sick, and Benny tried to call you Friday night, but I'm afraid he didn't get you. She is much better, but not out of the woods yet. She had a slight heart attack and pneumonia.*

Kelly, Clois and Mary Rose came Tuesday or Wednesday and they have helped sit with her. They left today. Ruth is here, but can't do much more than visit with her, which is a great help. She can call the nurses when she needs help. I'm not sure how I'll make out staying day and night, but I'm sure I'll make it.

One night Nannie was trying to get out of bed. She said she had to go to North Carolina "to get Mikie's baby." Later she asked me if Mikie was here, and I told her "no" but that I would call you. She said no, you mustn't leave the baby. Then she said "You know we found the baby in North Carolina." I hope this doesn't upset you, but I had to tell you what she said.   *Love, Mother*

March 8, 1976

Last Saturday, on an anonymous lead forwarded by California Living, Joe and I went to Merced and with the police checked out a house where someone had seen a little girl resembling Anna. Sure enough, there was a seven-year-old who closely resembled Anna, but wasn't her...a poignant scene.

CHAPTER FOURTEEN

The pages of the New Yorker may seem an odd place to obtain references for a private investigator. Our experience with private investigators, however, was limited to what we saw, in multiple image, on television, with one person standing outside (often in the rain) turning the antenna by hand while three others sat inside shouting instructions.

In November, 1978, a story by Calvin Trillin told about Josiah ("Tink") Thompson, a philosophy professor turned private detective, living near San Francisco. Trillin told of Tink's life as a Navy frogman with the Marines and as a Kierkegaard biographer and scholar at Haverford College.

In the sixties, Tink became known as an amateur investigator of the John F. Kennedy assassination and published a book, "Six Seconds in Dallas", which held that the Warren Commission's single-bullet theory was physically impossible. Discussing another case, Tink told Trillin "This is just the kind of case I really love. So much of it depends on logical analysis of the evidence. Really paying attention."

So we called him up and asked if he would take over the investigation of Anna's case, and he agreed. The details of his involvement are sketchy in my memory. I remember thinking that he was an unhurried, dynamic man who drove to the farm to talk at some length with us about what we knew, what we remembered. At the end of one conversation he told us that he was satisfied we had had nothing to do with Anna's disappearance. I remember being bewildered that he could have thought such a thing, and that he said families often were involved in child abductions.

Tink observed Anna's father for some time in 1978 and was of the opinion that he probably was not involved.

In January, 1980, Tink spent more time on the case, listening to amateur surveillance tapes Joe had made at the hotel in San Francisco where George Waters and George Brody were living. He listened to a taped interview with Craig Barrick, the carpenter who apparently was the last person on the farm to see Anna.

By this time, we had moved from the farm and were living in Montara, about 14 miles north. Tink wrote "Two weeks ago Nancy and I were driving down the coast. We drove up to the farm and looked around; the stream was high but not in flood. A lot of thinking, thinking---but no answers.

"Please let me know," he wrote, "if you would welcome the idea of talking once again about the case--at no charge. The case continues to tick in the back of my mind and I feel frustrated and disappointed that I was not able to open up any solid lead."

In 1988, Tink's book, Gumshoe, was published. In an interview in the San Francisco Chronicle, Tink said that solving cases "has to do with a Zen-like sense for the pace of action, so that 'the fingertip senses, hunch, intuition--that level of awareness is always much more important than deductive logic."

When I read the book, I learned about other cases Tink was working on at the time he was applying his intuition to our situation, among them a homicide and a child abduction.

However, in Anna's case, neither logic nor intuition yielded a clue.

March 22, 1979:HERE, THERE AND EVERYWHERE (GEOLOGY)

Joe, looking for information on Purisima Creek and its surroundings, called Dr. Dave Mustart, chairman of the Geology Department of San Francisco State University, who suggested he speak to geologist Kenneth R. Lajoie at the United States Department of the Interior in Menlo Park.

Joe's notes on March 22, 1979, say the following:

Purisima is still an active creek, with sediment continuously moving to the ocean. In high water extremes, it is possible to bury a car, for instance, with silt, but it would be uncovered the next spring or certainly the following winter.

The action of tides in winter tends to take sand and debris out and make sand bars which are brought back in by summer waves, to be redeposited on the beach.

Lajoie's opinion regarding a body falling into the creek: That it is possible a body could snag on something and be covered with silt, but he thought it would be more likely that it would be washed up on the banks by turbulent waters.

He was quite familiar with Purisima Creek, Joe said.

His opinion on aerial infra-red photography (to locate decomposing organic material) was that it showed ground water irregularities rather than heat emissions and would be an unlikely method for searching in silt, but possible.

Aerial photographs, using certain filters, might help locate a decomposing body.

A letter from Joe to Mr. Lajoie dated March 26 expands:

"I would like to thank you for your kind assistance. Your suggestions regarding the aerial photos were extremely helpful and your explanation of silting action in creeks was even more illuminating.

"I wonder if I might ask another favor of you? Since our child disappeared January 16, 1973, we have not discovered a clue as to her whereabouts. The San Mateo County Sheriff's Department has been most sympathetic and helpful from the beginning. Yet because of an initial assumption that our daughter fell into the creek, and even though after countless searches no evidence was ever discovered there, an attitude seems to pervade the Sheriff's office that "she's been silted over and might never be found" or "she probably got washed out to the ocean."

"A geological explanation of silting and ocean currents proffered by someone of your professional position and with an intimate knowledge of Purisima Creek itself would do much toward dispelling this attitude, which has of course slowed our very long search for our daughter. May I prevail upon you for such a written opinion? If so, and if you could send such a brief statement to me, my family and I will be most grateful for your efforts. Thank you again."

On May 1, 1979, Mr. Lajoie responded.

I apologize for the delay in responding to your letter of March 26, 1979. I have been away from the office a good deal and have been extremely busy while I am here.

As I mentioned to you on the telephone, my knowledge of Purisima Creek and its hydrology is general, not specific, so my comments are based on educated opinion, not fact.

Purisima Creek has incised or cut downward into its broad floodplain and formed a deep, narrow gully over the past 5,000-6,000 years. The narrow configuration of the present stream channel cut into bedroom indicates the stream is still eroding its bed, not depositing sediment. In this configuration alluvial material (silt, sand and gravel) eroded from the higher parts of the watershed are flushed through the lower parts of the stream channel. Sediment may be deposited in the stream bed temporarily, but is eventually washed out.

Purisima Creek, like all streams along the San Mateo Coast, has a very seasonal discharge pattern; floods occur during and after winter rains and the stream dries up during the late summer drought. To my knowledge Purisima Creek does not have a gauge so the exact winter discharge levels are not known. However, in my opinion, large objects such as rocks (maybe one to two feet in size) and logs, and large amounts of sediment can be moved during periods of high discharge (flood stage). Any sediment left in the stream channel after a flood would probably be washed out gradually over a period of days, weeks, months, or maybe the next year. Large objects such as branches, logs, etc., may get hung up in brush and log jams. Sediment may build up for longer periods of time behind persistent obstructions such as brush jams, but is eventually washed out.

I have never been in Purisima Creek during flood stage or even during normal winter flows, so I don't know the capability of the stream to move large objects through its channel and over the broad falls at the sea cliff. If logs get hung up on the falls where the flow broadens out, other large objects may get hung up there also. However, the few times I have seen the falls during the dry summer months, there were no logs hung up from the previous winter's floods. I hope these comments are of some use to you in your attempt to resolve the mystery surrounding your young daughter's disappearance in 1973. Please feel free to call again if you need further assistance obtaining or interpreting aerial photographs or maps.

CHAPTER FIFTEEN

Joseph Banks Rhine, 1895-1980, American psychologist, was a professor at Duke University from 1928 to 1965 and founded the Institute of Parapsychology at Durham, North Carolina, which he directed from 1964 to 1968. The letter his wife Louise wrote to her niece, Suzanne White, neighbor and friend of our family, on Feb. 23, 1973, included a strong caution with regard to psychics.

"I'm sorry this letter is going to be a disappointment to you, because when we got right down to it this morning we realized more clearly what I guess I actually knew that none of these West Coast psychic groups would be worth the time it would take to look them up. We find that the one I was thinking of in San Francisco is so loosely organized as far as we can tell that they don't have a headquarters and probably not a telephone.

"The truth is if we could have given you a name and if you could have gotten a medium recommended, the chances are next to nothing that it would have been anything but a run-around, and probably an expensive one. It's because we know this so well that we have never kept a list of mediums. Also the cases we've known of when one was called in to solve some mystery have never yielded anything worth while and often have raised false hopes and led to wild goose chases.

"Your mention of Tarot cards is another reminder of the superstition of the ages and does not give a one in a million chance of being meaningful. Most of the stories you hear about a medium who helped solve a crime are overdrawn and exaggerated.

"After all of our years studying parapsychology, we know the reason why. The psychic ability is real. But is an unconscious one. It has no identifying characteristic, so that there is no way of telling when a true "flash" comes through and when it's all just something made up in the unconscious, just like dreams are, and guesses, etc. And so JB and I decided that it would be no kindness to you or the mother to add this kind of thing to the tragedy even if we could have given you a contact. Such contacts may not even give you a sincere person, because charlatans are a dime a dozen, but even if the person is sincere and no matter how much he may believe in his ability, it still is no guarantee that he will be correct. And still farther, if he should tell something that happens to be correct, it still may not help in the locating of the child. In one such case of which I heard, the medium gave an identifying item about the child that only the parents knew, but nothing that helped them find him. It just added to their anxiety.

It was good to hear from you and I'm so sorry if your call netted you nothing...If any trace of the little girl is found, I hope I hear of it. It is hard not to help on a case like this but we have to decide that 'no help' is no better than none, if that makes sense."

This kindly advice notwithstanding, when there seemed no other place to look for Anna, we did consult various psychics. Sometimes friends urged us to go and even made appointments for us.

The Hallowed Grounds Fellowship of Spiritual Healing and Prayer, Santa Barbara, California, August 14th, 1973

"I thank you so much for your letter and am grieved to learn of your great sorrow in connection with your little daughter. What a terrible thing to have happen to you and herself. If I should get any sense psychically of her or her whereabouts I would let you know at once. In the meantime, we can only pray on a happy outcome of it all. All the laws of God and the Universe work out in justice and for this reason I have no doubt that you will eventually be restored to each other. Do please let us know whenever you may have any kind of news yourselves as like all your friends we are already praying with you.

"Keep that little garden of hers going and let it thrive and I say this because that area must already be serving as a focal point for all the earnest praying.

"I feel I am seeming to offer so little into your enquiries from me but the spirit friends of course know your request for help and as agents for God, you can be sure that behind the scenes they are working hard to bring you together again.

Please accept the fact of my very deep feeling of sympathy.
Yours sincerely, George Daisley

Association for Research and Enlightenment, Inc., Virginia Beach, Virginia. Hugh Lynn Cayce, President.

"I apologize for not answering your letter sooner.
I have heard good reports of some of Gerard Croiset's work. However, he is besieged on every hand and it is most difficult to get in touch with him. His address is......Holland. You certainly might try writing him direct.
I sincerely hope that it will be possible for him to give you some help. Frankly it is a remote possibility at this point. I think time, space and dimensions are all involved here."

March 7, 1974, notes from an hour's conversation with the Rev. Pearl Shannon, arranged by Byron Edelen. She produced some unusual things, since as far as I know she was not expecting me (I was taking someone else's appointment). Before I had told her our names, she said my husband was not Anna's father, that we thought Anna had gone into the water, that Anna had curly hair and was fearless, independent, happy, healthy, and motherly toward me. She said, in brief, that George, Anna's father, was "cracked". That Anna had been "stolen" by a woman in her late thirties who had observed her actions for some time and walked "along the bank of the water, on sand, held out her hand, and walked off with her."

She said that the woman had a relationship with George and that he had exploited her need and inability to have a child in directing her to take Anna. That Anna was stolen with George's knowledge, if not his physical assistance. She thought there was some link with Kansas or Oklahoma, but thought Anna was in California, northern or Baja, in a semi-rural arid place where people speak "with a drawl." She said she was over-protected, "smotheringly" tended. That she was healthy but confused because of the uprooting. That I should write the Examiner to establish a "point of contact". "The first time my guides have ever told me that," she said.

She said George's motivation was vindictive: "If I can't have her, she can't have her either." That Anna is highly sensitive to psychic forces and may be approached in this way. That there was no trace or indication that Anna was "out of the body". "She's alive, in the body, no doubt about it," she said. "It would be easier for me to tell you she isn't," she said, "but that's not true."

She said to maintain a loving connection, spoke of "God's time" and a "karmic pattern." Said the loss was harder on me than on Anna, who was "very old." She said "You can't be so obsessed with your anguish that you forget to live."

There was more, but that's the crux of it. She was a sympathetic woman.

(No date or point of origin)
From the desk of Nancy French

Your letter written to the Reverend Rauscher has been referred to me to answer. You asked in your letter for any intuition regarding her disappearance. My intuition is this: that she is all right. My seeing of her is a healthy child, light skin, pink dress with some blue in it, long hair light and shiny. I see her in a country setting with people just passing middle age. I feel she was taken or as you said "abducted". I see a New England type church. Did she enjoy church when she was with you? Her ability to be openly loving is an asset to her.

Now, you have my blessings in handling the anxiety you must have. Continue to keep your faith but also keep on building a good life for yourself. Do as much as you can to have a normal life. Learn to live with your loss. I am not saying you may or may not see Anna, but in any case you should continue in a good life as much as you can. I will be attended the S.F.F. Annual Conference and the Carleton College Retreat. If you are at either and care to talk with me, let me know. You are welcome to write too. Blessings, N.George

---

Rev. Grace Forman, Lily Dale, New York, May 24, 1975

In reply to your recent letter, I was disappointed that you did not send an article that your daughter Anne had touched. The vibration would have been stronger. I felt that you had laundered the article you sent. I will return the tape recording when I have a chance to play it as we do not have a small recorder but a friend has kindly offered to bring hers.

I was looking for a hair ribbon or something Anne had worn that did not have too much value.

I do feel Anne (sic) is alive and living in Sacramento, California, in a small white house with a small porch on it and dark trimming, could be brown or black. Near the house is tall grass growing and sand around it. Anne was picked up by a couple in a blue car. They wanted a child but did not have one. The man jumped out of the car and left the engine running and put Anne between them. Anne was screaming and crying but they did not stop.

I see boats and feel many make a living fishing.

Anne goes to school and I feel perhaps you could look at the children at their recess time. If she sees you I see her run to you calling "Mama." If you have a small article such as a hair ribbon, I would appreciate your sending it.

I do not feel Anne has been abused in any way.

The name Gary came in to me; I do not know if it is a street or a first name of the man.

May God bless you and send his angels to you to help you in finding Anne.

Church of Divine Man
Berkeley Psychic Institute, November 18, 1980

Notes from a tape of poor quality recall a language used by the three "readers" which was so esoteric it was hard to make much of it. Their reading was concerned with what they saw of my aura and chakras and was interspersed with yawns, laughter and humming, which seemed to have something to do with their ways of keeping their own energy up. The readers claimed to see "a cemetery picture out in front of you" and also "suicide pictures". They also said they saw an image of a lighthouse with a searchlight. They said there was a cross in the aura.

(No date)

Patricia-Rochelle Diegel, Montara, used Tarot cards to give a reading of "past lives". She said I had had 396 earth lives, 102 male and 294 female, as well as a life on Hauwara in the Fifth Dimension.. These included "Selenah" in Atlantis in 21,100 B.C. She said I was a sculptor whose mother was Aziza, whose sister was Susan, and whose brother was John. In another life, she said, I was named Mizu, lived in Egypt in 3600 B.C., was an entertainer whose father was Nonda. After that, she said, I was named Mary, lived in the Holy Land in 500 B.C., was a healer; my sister was Cynthia and my daughter was Frances. I saved the life of someone named Robert. As Olivia, I lived in Rome in 200 A.D., was involved somehow with the arts, was married to Sam and had as children Edward and Nonda. In 1500 A.D. I was named Eleana, lived in Spain and England, was an ambassador's daughter who was married to Nonda, whose father was George, and who had five children including Tommy and Erin. Then I was Suzette, lived in France in 1700 A.D. and traveled to the United States with my husband. Frances was my companion and Edward was my son. I did needlepoint in Kentucky.

A computer-generated astrological chart for Anna Waters, no date, but copyrighted 1972 by the American Astrological Association.

Born in longitude 122.00 degrees west, latitude 37.00 degrees north on September 25, 1967 at local time 16:44.
Planetary conditions at birth:
Sun 01 degrees of Libra
Ascendant 03 degrees of Pisces
Moon 22 degrees of Gemini
Venus 28 degrees of Leo
Mercury 24 degrees of Libra
Mars 10 degrees of Sagittarius
Jupiter 25 degrees of Leo
Saturn 09 degrees of Aries
Neptune 22 degrees of Scorpio
Uranus 25 degrees of Virgo
Pluto 20 degrees of Virgo.

The computer readout gave many suggestions including "Your fate will be very two sided as you will go from bad to good periods very quickly. You should try to apply your mental energy to constructive work such as teaching.

Around April 20, 1975 a neighbor did a progressed chart for January 16, 1973, incorporating Anna's chart with those of her parents and stepfather. She saw no aspect of accident or death anywhere, she said. She noted "extraordinary worship" of Anna by her father. My chart showed unusual susceptibility in the area of home and children.

Paraphrased from Solar Biology, Hiram E. Butler:

Libra is the third sign of the reproductive trinity and is a cardinal air sign. Its special gift is the ability to maintain balance and justice in all situations. Its challenge is toward the perfect intellect; therefore its complimentary sign is Aries. Its color is green, its musical tone is F sharp or G flat, its fellow air signs Aquarius and Gemini, its friends Virgo and Scorpio, and its fellow cardinal signs Aries, Cancer and Capricorn.

Libra with the moon in Gemini is produced by unsatisfactory conditions or surroundings, with obstacles in the way of the prosperity of the parents. It gives the child a restless, active mind and adapts it to intellectual and educational spheres. It gives the child high aspirations and ability in arts, mechanics and mathematics. It increases the liability of going to extremes.

Mercury in Gemini helps quiet nervous, restless tendencies and creates a strong, studious mind inclined toward scientific studies, especially of mathematics and physics.

Venus in Libra confers a passionate nature and fine intuitions. It forms a harmonious link between the intuition and reasoning faculties. It strengthens the generative function and increases the love of beauty.

Mars in Cancer finds its native home, where it gives the strongest parental love and love of children in general. It greatly increases the domestic qualities and often overpowers other strong tendencies. It confers love of agricultural life and animals.

Jupiter in Aquarius creates activities with other people, a love of public live, and an inclination toward politics.

Saturn in Libra is a harmonious position and contributes intuitive power, a visionary nature, and a tendency toward mechanical genius. In the higher order of humanity it gives intuition concerning a nobler state of social and domestic life, and it contributes order and harmony to the mental faculties in general.

Uranus in Pisces imparts a strong desire to study and investigate everything relating to the unseen forces in the universe. It increases a person's secretiveness and gives a restless activity to the mind.

CHAPTER SIXTEEN

January 18, 1977

Sunday it was four years since Anna disappeared and Joe gave me a little portrait of her which he had commissioned our neighbor Howard Gilligan to do. I worked a little in the garden today and gave two drakes to the little boys next door.

(Painting of Anna by Howard Gilligan)

San Francisco, March 12, 1977
I remember the birth of your Anna, and did not know from newspaper reports of the tragedy of her disappearance. I told (my brother, your science teacher) of what happened and his comment was that you had achieved the success of sanity--he speaks of you with great admiration and praise.
Sincerely, Irene C. (obstetrician's nurse)

Joe Ford secretly observed George Waters and George Brody on several occasions, parking his truck and watching their comings and goings. His transcribed notes give an idea of these sessions.

March 22, 1979: 5:25 P.M. George and a woman come out of MHC (probably Mission Neighborhood Health Center, 240 Shotwell, San Francisco). Woman gets in the car and they drive off. I proceed to Hotel Paul.

     6:15: GW arrives at Hotel. Parks. Gets back in and drives off.

     6:30: GW returns, enters hotel.

March 23, 1979, Friday: Similar observations at Hotel.

March 24, 1979, Saturday: 8:45 A.M., GW and Brody exit hotel. I took pictures.

     10:35 A.M., Brody comes back to hotel on foot and enters.

March 27, 1979: 5:32 P.M., MHC. GW departs southbound on 16th, then left on Harrison

     11:05 P.M., Hotel Paul: GW arrives alone with paper bag and enters hotel.

     11:37 P.M. GW and Brody exit the hotel.

     12:30 A.M.: Both return to hotel.

March 28, 1979: 2:10 P.M. Car in lot at MHC.

     4 P.M. MHC, car in lot.

March 30, 1979: 5:32 P.M., MHC. Set up camera. GW comes out alone, drove East on 16th toward Harrison. I went directly to Hotel Paul. No car there.

     6 P.M. Saw Brody coming down 16th Street.

March 31, 1979: 6:30 A.M. Hotel Paul. Camera set up.

Surveillance photograph of Brody, Waters, 1974

8:30 A.M. GW and Brody both come out, GW carrying a small canvas bag. Brody stops to talk to a street girl from the Temple Parking Garage. She appears to know him well. GW kept walking to car. Flat tire. Drove away

4-1-79 (?) 11 A.M., Brody comes back to Hotel Paul with newspaper.

April 2, 1979: 12:45 P.M., MHC, no car in lot or on street.

(Transcribed from undated recording Joe made during observations)

..on Van Ness--two blocks, and I lost him...don't know where he was heading so I went back to Zim's and fiddled around to see if maybe he went to dinner, but I didn't see him there or his car, so now I'm parked over across the street from the Hotel Paul. I'm gonna try this tape recording stuff to see if listening to it in the morning on my way to work will help me center on what happened while I'm down. I'm running into this fog here. The more I come down here, the farther away it seems to get. (Sigh) Sure is weird downtown.

If I can get a key, rent a room, find out where 206 is located, rent an apartment on the second floor...have a master (key) made up. It must be possible; people get locked out...find out how a lock works, there's the best bet. Fooling around with George and Brody and the manager seems somewhat scary, too melodramatic for me. I can find out how it's done by calling locksmiths, telling them I'm locked out.

An old man coming out of the hotel, looks something like Brody, white hair, heading down towards Jones, kinda staggering I wonder if it is Brody. I think I'll get out and check. I t looked like him a lot, bowed legs, grey hair, hat, came out of the Hotel Paul, walked back on Geary the opposite way for about a block, disappeared...I realized I'd lost him, turned around and came back but then picked him up again...went left on Jones...saw him go up the stairs at the Hotel Shawmet on O'Farrell Street at Jones. The sign says No Visitors...closes at 8 o'clock. Maybe it was he and maybe not.

Paul Hotel, 630 Geary Street, Geary and Jones. George and Brody are reported to have room 206. I think I'll stay here tonight and tomorrow after work I'll go to the San Mateo library and get a book on

locksmithing, see if I can figure out how to do it myself

The man I originally followed coming out of the.....hotel just staggered back in. I'm not sure whether it's Brody or not. It didn't really look like it was. I don't know who it was I followed to the Shawmet Hotel; maybe it was Brody, maybe it wasn't.

Five after ten. Just had some coffee. ....should be pulling in almost any time now. Still no sign of Brody. There's the car. He'll probably go around the block.. The time is ten twenty-nine. I'm going to get out and take a walk. He's stopping up there at the corner. Parked around the corner. Looks like he may be gonna walk back to the hotel. He made a right on Leavenworth. I'll be watching. Nothing yet. Nothing yet. (Sigh). He stopped at the corner store to get ...I'm going to get out. Leavenworth and..... right on the corner...looks like a temporary...(inaudible)

Eleven o'clock. Headin' home. Gonna swing by Van Ness and Geary, see if anybody's there.

September 9, 1979

    At church, Kelly Peterson, who was one of Anna's best friends, and her mother visited from Belmont. Kelly was taller than I! Pastor Tom announced that I was pregnant. After church, Mrs. Peterson came up to me with tears in her eyes and said that Kelly had said "Oh, that's Anna's mother. Anna's going to have a sister!"

October 5, 1979

Friday, full moon in Libra. At about 4:30 this afternoon I lost the baby.

November 29, 1979

On Tuesday we went to see Kathlyn Rhea, a psychic, who said Anna went into the creek and was killed when her head hit the rocks.

September 6, 1980

Today at the grocery store, I ran into Mrs. B., who lived at Martin's Beach and whose daughter, Becky, was Anna's best friend in kindergarten. A soft-faced woman with kind eyes. I hardly dared look at the young girl with her, because I knew it would be Becky. They didn't recognize me. She was as tall as I am, with dark serious eyes, a woman. I don't think I would have known her except that I recognized her mother first.

In 2006, Anna's friend Kelly said that she had attended a 20th high school reunion and had learned that Becky had died the previous year.

September 26, 1980

I always await and expect miracles on my birthday (or any time I need them, for that matter) and yesterday for Anna's 13th birthday I had a few, so subjective and personal that I doubt they would have had any significance for anyone but me.

Early in the morning I drove in the fog to San Francisco for my piano lesson with Mr. Sheldon, and he presented me with copies of the Pastoral Songs to which he wrote the music and I wrote the lyrics. I played for him Schumann's untitled pieces from "Album for the Young", about which Clara Schumann said to her daughter Eugenie that "Papa was perhaps writing of things parents think about their children."

I came home to a room full of flowers which Arnie brought from the fields Wednesday and played the Pastoral Songs. One, "The Walking Place", was meant to be Purisima Canyon, where Anna and I used to walk, and hearing it made me cry.

THE WALKING PLACE

Years have softened the rocky face of the road,
This place where mosses remember to grow,
And where the rose, escaped and wild,
Leads the thin hard life of the vagabond.
Trillium, wide, watched us as children
And went home with us to perish in comfort
And bloomed once again till paths worn smooth
Became our diary.
Here this adventure befell us, and there...
Who walked? Who was walked upon?
What strange thread was woven throughout our way?

In the evening, Les called and I got to speak to my niece Mikie, "It's Auntie Mikie! Hello, Auntie Mikie!" who demanded that I come and visit her, and Aloha, who insisted that I talk to her as long as I had talked to her twin.

My day was filled with other people's daughters--almost if someone or something had lent me dozens of little girls to abate the grief of the one I lost.

And that is what I meant by miracles.

October 6, 1980

At Choir School tonight, the pastor's son, age four, asked it were true that I had a daughter and she got lost. Taking a deep breath, I said yes, and answered an onslaught of questions. How old was she? How long ago was it? How old would she be now? Did you call the police? Was it on the news? What was her name? Are they still looking for her? Do you have some boys? Were they upset? Where were they when it happened?

One little girl said "Stephen Stainer was lost and they didn't know where he was and he came back after seven years."

Another child said "Maybe she was kidnapped. Did the police say she was kidnapped?"

Yet another said "I wish I could go and find her for you."

And another said "If she came back, I know you'd be awfully happy."

Then I reminded Nicole that she was lost once, but got found...and said that it seems as if it is hard for us not to know the answer to something because we like to understand...and that we could talk about it any time they wanted to, but that we'd better sing some songs now.

October 16, 1980

Last night, teaching the children the song which puts the books of the New Testament to melody, I said that my sister always said "FLIP-yuns, KLOSS-yans" for Philippians, Colossians, and Troy, stuttering, said "Did your sister disappear from the back yard or the front yard?"

Unwilling to get into it again, I asked him (kindly, I hope) to talk to me about it after class. I don't want them to associate me permanently with tragedy.

July 1, 1981

Tony's voice on the telephone was choked. There had been an automobile accident in northern Greece. His 12-year-old daughter Marina had been killed. His 15-year-old daughter Antigone had been flown to New York for neurosurgery at Columbia Presbyterian Hospital, where George had received his medical training. I had no words. I cried over the telephone, 10,000 miles from where it had happened, until finally we said goodbye. Much later, Tony told me that his wife, Elli, had said "Call Mikie". Her first words after the accident. Antigone would recover.

CHAPTER SEVENTEEN

January 19, 1982

Joe came home last night after spending four hours looking through George's papers at his brother Bill's in the east Bay. The circumstances of George's death are as strange as those of his life. They found his body at the Abbey or Abby Hotel (formerly the Paul Hotel) in San Francisco. An inquest is being held, but the body has already been cremated (and in fact was unceremoniously dumped, the ashes, that is, on a table by his brother Bill last night in Joe's presence. "Here's George.")

The room in which his body was found was sealed, but there is another room in the same hotel and possibly an apartment down the street used by Brody and George which have not been sealed or searched, to my knowledge. They seem to have used several different names, Post Office boxes, and addresses. We know this from investigations conducted by Detective Maguire and by Tink and later by Joe, who did various illegal things to check out the possibility that George was involved in Anna's disappearance.

As a result of these investigations, we all thought that George and Brody were strange and that the strangeness itself seemed suspicious, but that there was no proof that they were involved with Anna. At one point, Joe drilled a hole in the wall of the next-door closet at the hotel, inserted a microphone, and tape-recorded a conversation in which George said "I'm glad the tot died."

I think Bill and Laana are tired, busy, and overwhelmed by all this. They mentioned that George had taken out many life insurance policies. They gave us the file cabinet with George's remaining papers (many had been destroyed, apparently by George, before his body was found), but there was nothing we could link directly with Anna's disappearance. In a safe deposit box, they found one letter I had written to George and the article from California Living, nothing else.

There was a receipt for a passport application dated May 3, 1975, as well as receipts for child support, for student loan repayments.

Joe's notes say the following:

Bill Waters was contacted by the San Francisco Coroner's Office early Monday, Jan. 11, 1982, and informed of George Waters' death. At that point the body in the Abby Hotel had been dead three to seven days, putting the date of death between Jan. 4 and Jan. 8 (the death certificate says Jan. 7.) Bill and a friend went to the Abby Hotel and collected all records and personal effects. Bill spoke with the San Francisco Coroner, who released George's body for cremation. The Coroner said that it appeared to be a death by poison and that a suicide note was left by George (and still possessed by the Coroner's office.)

It appeared through Bill's search of records that George Brody had had terminal cancer and had been treated through various legitimate and pseudo-legitimate clinics and had been under intensive home care by George Waters, including tube feeding.

There is a report dated December 29, 1981, Public Administrator's Investigation, regarding George Brody. It lists a birth date for Brody of August 15, 1923 (surely false) and Massachusetts as birthplace. It says the decedent, "a friend of Dr. Waters for years", had no income, never worked, supposedly was involved in politics at one time. "Searched decedent's room, found no papers, no social security number," the report said.

I believe the Coroner told Bill that he thought there was something weird about a doctor living in the same hotel signing a death certificate. (George Brody's death certificate lists as "unknown" date of birth, age, birth name of mother and father, occupation, social security number, occupation. The address is given as Abby Hotel, 630 Geary Street, Room 407. George Waters stated on the death certificate that he had attended the deceased since January, 1968. His own address he gave as P. O. Box 5884, San Francisco. The body was cremated December 30, 1981 at Evergreen Cemetery, Oakland.

January 20, 1982

Joe checked out an address given for George Brody on George Waters' passport, 1156 Sutter Street, Hotel Otis. The building at that address was remodeled in 1980 and all previous tenants are gone.

January, 1982, Joe interviews the desk clerk at the Abby Hotel:

Joe Ford: I stayed at your hotel for a while under the name of Boger.

Clerk: Under the name of what?

J: Boger.

C: Oh, you're the truck driver, bus driver or something. That's right. I remember you. How are you?

J: O.K. Do you have a couple of minutes to talk, or are you in the middle of something?

C: No, go right ahead.

J: O. K., let me lay a little story on you right off the bat. The two Georges. George Brody and George Waters, who died.

C: Yes.

J: Well, I don't know if you ever noticed it, but I was very interested in their activities. And I'll tell you why. I married his ex-wife. George Waters' ex-wife.

C: Really.

J: Yes.

C: He's a doctor at Kaiser.

J: Yes, he was.

C: And his brother's a doctor.

J: His brother's a doctor, right. Our daughter was missing, disappeared about seven years ago. And all this time we haven't found a trace of her yet. It seemed that he was a very likely person to possibly be involved in it. That was my motive for going down there and trying to be close to them to see if they had any connection.

C: You know, when the old man died, Christmas eve, he died in the fellow's room and that's when I found out he was a doctor, and a doctor at Kaiser, too. Then he committed suicide.

J: Yes, we were contacted by the brother, who is still close to the family, and he gave us some of that information, but I was wondering if I could ask you a couple of things about it.

C: But there is nothing I can tell you; it's so secretive.

J: Just a couple of basic things like which room was it that Brody died in. Were you there when they called the coroner?

C: Oh, sure, of course.

J: Was it the fourth floor room?

C: No, Brody lived in 407. He died in 206, in Waters' room.

J: O.K., you know what it seemed to me; like they were really living in 206 and 407.

C: I'm sure it was a Father-Son complex. Oh, I know it was. He had tears in his eyes. He said "You'll never know how much that old man meant to me. Well, that old man used to screech and scream. 'You...S.O.B., and the guy would never open his mouth. I mean, a doctor living here in this hotel...

J: What happened (the night Brody died). I'm looking for little details. Did the coroner show up that night?

C: Yes.

J: Christmas eve night, the 24th, when Brody died.

C: Just a minute. (To someone else) Do you remember when Brody died? It was on a weekend; that was Christmas eve. But they didn't come till Monday, did they?
(To J.) No, they didn't come till Monday. (Changes mind and says the body was removed that same day.)

J: So they came that very evening and took his body off to somewhere?

C: Yes. Then a week or more later, I...went upstairs and they had three chains on the door of which I only had two keys, so I called the police to witness me entering their room.

J: Really. Did you think something had gone wrong?

C: Yes, of course, and there he (Waters) sat, fully dressed in this recliner chair, not a hair on his head ruffled.

J: Is that right?

C: Was dead.

J: And I understand there was a glass beside him with crystals in it or something.

C: Yes, was a bottle. There was a glass turned upside-down, but there was a bottle. Yes, it was a shock to everybody. You know, he really warmed up to me because he was lonely, I guess; before, he was so distant and secretive...He said the old man he knew had some wealthy relatives somewhere back East, but he had no idea where. He didn't even have the keys for his safety deposit box.

J: The old man had a safety deposit box and he didn't have the keys for it.

C: The young man didn't have it; that's how secretive they were even to each other. Found strange notes in the room about complexes, guilt complexes...you know, they have been here about five years. I've been here the first of September three years. I was manager.

J: They have been here ten years. They were here when it was owned by the Indian family.

C: Yes, the Patels.

J: Right, well, let me ask you this; I'm trying to work out some of these details. When Brody did die, when the old man died, did George move a bunch of stuff out or anything like that?...

C: No, there was boxes of hats that had been cleaned and blocked back in 1980, boxes after boxes of hats, shoes, shirts, underwear, and the brother came, gave me some of it and the balance gave to the Salvation Army.

J: They never had any people come in, did they?

C: Never. They never got a message on the phone here. They never got a piece of mail. They had their own phone.

J: What a mystery. What a sad situation....I wonder how old (Brody) was. How old would you say he was? About 68?

C: Oh, no; he was in his seventies.

J: It must be strange. You live with people or live next door all these years.

C: We called them the Odd Couple, you know.

J: Who paid the rent, by the way?

C: Brody always paid it.

J: He paid the rent on both units.

C: I don't know where the money came from. He came in and paid the rents.

J: Did he pay it in cash?

C: Always in cash, and always in small bills; stand there counting out over and over, so finicky, you know.

J: Did you see that note that (George Waters) left?

C: Yes.

J: Did you get a chance to read it?

C: There was two or three notes. It wasn't like a death note he had left. There was things pinned on the wall about guilt complexes and just weird things like that...

J: It wasn't a suicide note?

C: No...you know they were listed here under the name of Walters.

J: Yes, I knew that.

March 4, 1983: Joe Ford tries hypnotic regression back to the day Anna disappeared. The tapes from this session are almost inaudible, the name of the hypnotist was not recorded, and no useful information came out of the session except possibly that Anna had visited another friend, Kelly, the day before she went missing. (She had two friends named Kelly, but I do not remember her visiting either one on Jan. 15.)

Hypnotist: You're going to go back in time a day, a week, a month, a year...five years, ten years...to Christmas of 1972. It's an old yellow house. What can you see? What presents did you get? Speak, even though you're deeply asleep. Anna and the boys were there, opening the presents.

It's New Year's now. Do you remember New Years? You don't remember.
Joe: Mikie made some bread.

Hypnotist: Stop trying. Let it happen. Go back to Christmas day. Was there anything unusual about the day? (Sigh) Stop trying so hard. What presents did you buy?

Joe: (inaudible)....

Hypnotist: What's the room where you eat the bread on New Year's?

Joe: Fireplace....

Hypnotist: It's the day before Anna vanished. What day of the week was it?

Joe: Monday.

Hypnotist: What happened that morning? What time did you get up?

Joe: 6:30.
Hypnotist: What did you do? Put your pants on...yeah...yeah ... so it was raining. What did you do? Went to work? Where'd you work? On the ranch? Your wife stayed home? You were gone all day?

What happened then? Came home. Drove down to the ranch...parked your truck. Was it dark or light?

Joe: Light.

Hypnotist: How do you feel?

Joe: Happy to have a day off.

Hypnotist: Then what happened?

(Can't hear Joe's answers at all)

Hypnotist: Anna say anything about anything unusual?

Joe:... a friend of Suzanne's, a fellow who worked with me.... I fell asleep. ...calling for Anna, calling out the back door...down the path and through the gate to Suzanne's house...calling for Anna...Did you go to Kelly's house? No. Far away.

Hypnotist: It's about 2 in the afternoon.

Joe: Went across the bridge....

  The session with the hypnotist revealed very little. However, Joe's undated notes are a concise summary of January 16, 1973:
  Weather: Bad storms lashed the Coastside area east of Half Moon Bay Tuesday morning, resulting in a blackout for Half Moon Bay on Tuesday afternoon. It lasted one hour, ten minutes. Cold and wet.

  January 16, 1973, Tuesday
7 A.M. Joe to work, then to Palo Alto
7:30 Kids off to school. Rained heavy
  Mikie did chores circa 10 A.M. Came back. Wrote poem. In middle of poem Mikie heard screams--ran down to bridge--Quinn's wife Sandy had been attacked by Hulk. Mikie brought her back up to house. She called husband to come shoot rooster. He refused. She

was there to feed the horses before the blacksmith came. He had reputation for hot head.

Arlene/Asya came circa 11 A.M.
Joe came home circa 12 noon.
Anna came home on school bus circa 1 P.M. Went to room. Changed clothes. Changed to play clothes--vinyl boots. Asya/Arlene left. Suzy came in circa 1:30. Craig arrived 2:15. Recollects later passing white panel truck with young man/old man. waved to him. They were going west.
Five minutes later, 2:20, A. is missed. Search started.
3 P.M. Sheriff called.
3:15: Charlene Machado hears noise and siren east of house.
3:15: Sheriff arrives, sounds siren.

Occam's Razor: When seeking a hypothesis, one should first examine the least astonishing possibility. If I proceed by Occam's principle, the law of least astonishment would lead me to surmise that Anna drowned in Purisima Creek on Jan. 16, 1973, but we have never found any evidence that Anna went into the creek, and the evidence around the Anna's father and his companion is sketchy.

I have had to conclude that my own intuition, such as it is, doesn't help much. It is interesting when I have an idea and it proves to be true, but I am wrong as often as I am right. I had no intuition at the time of Anna's disappearance except that she was absent from the scene. I led everyone to the creek not because I thought or felt she went into the creek, but because the creek was the most immediate danger of the various possibilities, the one which gave us the least amount of time to save her.

In the days after Christmas of 1981, and before I had received the telephone call regarding his death, I had a few thoughts regarding George which I dismissed at the time as sentimental recollections. One was in the course of copying my old Greek records onto tape. I came across a record of "Tonight We Improvise" which contained a theatrical monologue which George used to recite. It was a vivid memory. I could almost hear him say the words. I believe the words are from Pirandello, with music by Manos Hadjidaki.

(Translated from Greek)
The performance isn't lights,
Isn't the scenery.
It is the people, you and me.
It is the women who ask questions;
It is the children who look at us.
And so you and I
Let the hour go all by itself.
The performance isn't lights,
Isn't the scenery.
It is the people, you and me.
It is your participation
In our loneliness.
It is your breathing in our silence,
And finally, it is your love for us.

The other lyric I came across on this same day was from the movie "Phaedra", and I could almost hear George singing it. The song was by Greek composer Mikis Theodorakis, set to a poem by Nikos Gatsos.

In the other world you'll go to,
Watch out not to become a cloud
In the bitter white of daybreak,
Lest you be recognized by your mother,
Who is cleaning at the door.
I sprinkled you with rose-water.
You sprinkled me with poison.

These impressions occurred on about December 29, 1981. On Sunday, Jan. 17, for no apparent reason, I played the beautiful "Pie Jesu" from the Gabriel Faure Requiem at church, thinking that it was inappropriate for the second Sunday after Epiphany, but that nobody would recognize it. ("Blessed Jesus, Lord, give to them eternal rest.") On Sunday afternoon, Laana, George's brother's wife, called and told me about George's death.

Someone who believed in psychic phenomena would interpret these things as some kind of evidence. I no longer have much faith at all in psychic phenomena, but I will allow an "if...then" in this instance. I don't need to spell it out, really.

January 20, 1982

This clipping arrived in a note from Anna's grandmother today.

Dr. George Henry Waters II, 42, son of Mrs. Anna Waters and the late Dr. Henry Waters, died Monday in San Francisco. Memorial services and burial will take place in San Francisco.

Dr. Waters was born April 14, 1939, in Iloilo, Philippines. He graduated from Taft School, Watertown, Conn., and received his bachelor of arts degree in 1961 from Princeton University, Princeton, N. J. On June 1, 1966, he received his doctor of medicine degree from the College of Physicians and Surgeons, Columbia University, New York City.

Between college and medical school he taught for one year at the American Farm School, Salonika, Greece. He practiced medicine in San Francisco.

Survivors include his mother; a brother, Dr. William Waters, San Francisco; and a sister, Mary-Alice Waters, New York City.

His father, Dr. Henry Waters, died Oct. 11, 1975.

In the Jan. 24 New Yorker, there is a quotation from Satayana in a reference to William Alfred's new play, "The Curse of an Aching Heart". "Everything in nature is lyrical in its ideal essence, tragic in its fate, and comic in its existence. Being, then, is the dazzle each of us makes as we thread the dance of those three rhythms of our lives."

There was a small memorial service in San Francisco for George, which I attended. I gave a small carved Philippine box of his to his brother, Bill. When the University Cottage Club at Princeton class observed its 100th anniversary in 1986 (and admitted women for the first time) I sent George's old-fashioned draw plane to the University Cottage Club for their memorial display, along with a quote from Verse Seventy-Four of the Tao Te Ching:

Trying to cut wood like a master carpenter,
You cannot avoid cutting your hand.

It was this draw plane George used to make the bed which was later recycled into other furniture, the dining room table and benches which I still use, the redwood chest which still holds Anna's clothes, and Anna's cradle and high chair.

After a service at the Cottage Club which George's mother, Ann, attended, a memorial service was held at the chapel at Princeton.

CHAPTER EIGHTEEN

By 1984, we had exhausted all reasonable efforts (as well as many unreasonable efforts) to find Anna. We gave all our information to the fledgling National Center for Missing and Exploited Children, and it felt to us as if they were taking up the search at the point where our energies and resources were exhausted.

Ever since that time, the National Center has each month distributed photographs of Anna to periodicals and organizations. When the technology became available, the National Center asked for pictures of members of the family at the age of twenty-five, and they produced an age-advanced photograph of Anna as she might have looked at that age.

In 1973, we did not hear much about missing children. There was no national network to provide information on the subject, and cases which appeared in the news seemed to be random, isolated instances. After 24 hours, parents of a missing child could file a Missing Persons report. The Federal Bureau of Investigation could be called in only if there was hard evidence that a child had been taken out of state or if there was a ransom note.

Although legislation regarding kidnapping really started after the Lindbergh kidnapping case in 1932, no rigorous support for families of children missing for whatever reason was available for decades after this time.

In 1974, Congress passed the Juvenile Justice and Delinquency Prevention Act which gave certain rights and protection to runaway children. In 1980, an amendment to this act provided seed money to establish and operate community-based programs to provide shelter and assistance to homeless children.

By 1984, the abduction and murder of Adam Walsh, the series of child murders in Atlanta, the serial murders of runaway children in Texas, the "Minnesota Connection" of runaways to the streets of New York City alerted the country to the vulnerability of its children.

David Collins, the father of Kevin Collins, who was kidnapped in February, 1984, said in an interview that there are eight to ten thousand child abductions every year.

In October 1984, Congress began to change the direction of the JJDP act by amending the Act to incorporate the Missing Children's Assistance Act. Congress recognized that "in many cases, parents and local law enforcement officials have neither the resources nor the expertise to mount expanded search efforts."

In about February of 1985, FBI director William H. Webster ordered field agents to notify FBI headquarters about all cases of missing children without requiring proof of interstate travel or a ransom note, saying that "interstate travel can be presumed after 24 hours from the time the minor was abducted or missing under circumstances indicating an abduction."

By March, 1985, regional organizations offering assistance in missing children cases included the following: The Adam Walsh Child Resource Center in Winter Park, Florida, Child Find-Missouri, Child Find-Utah, Children's Rights of New York, Children's Rights of Pennsylvania, Child Save of Concord, California, Childseekers of Rutland, Vermont and fifty others in the United States and Canada.

A pamphlet circulated by the United States Department of Justice in 1986 categorized types of missing children: Nonfamily or stranger abduction, family abduction (usually by a noncustodial spouse), runaway children (those who voluntarily abandon parents or other legal guardians), and throwaway children--those who are either abandoned or forced out of their homes by parents or legal guardians.

"A common thread", the pamphlet said, "running through all cases of missing children is the danger of physical and emotional injury and the threat of sexual exploitation to children who are out of lawful and caring custody. The longer children are gone from their homes, the greater the probability that (1) they will not be reunited with a family in a stable home environment and (2) they will be victimized on the streets."

At the time the National Center was founded, there was only one state clearing house for missing persons. By 1989, the Center had helped create forty more.

Today, parents of a missing child only have to access the World Wide Web by computer to instigate an international search. Through the National Center's home page, a parent can type in a description of the child and the name of the local police authorities. Within minutes, an amazing network of resources is available including an international bureau which works within the parameters of the Hague Convention, an agreement on child abduction which by 1996 had been signed by 187 nations and principalities.

There is an international service of the NCMEC at www.icmec.org which focuses on children who may have been taken to countries other than those in which they were born. The organization says "Our campaign against international child abduction takes a leadership role in supporting the Hague Convention and making it easier to implement."

The National Center's services include hotlines to assist parents and professionals, photo distribution, project alert, the age progression program, and case management. Their services to me personally have also included invitations to participate in media events publicizing cases of missing children, research projects on missing children, many telephone calls, and general support, access, and sympathy. Considering the sad fact that many families of missing children become terribly isolated in their grief, the contact alone has inestimable value.

NCMEC, according to its literature, spearheads national efforts to locate and recover missing children and attempts to raise public awareness about ways to prevent child abduction, molestation, and sexual exploitation. It is a private, nonprofit organization which operates under a Congressional mandate and works in conjunction with the United States Department of Justice's Office of Juvenile Justice and Delinquency Prevention.

Since its founding, the Center has taken more than a million calls on its national hotline, 1-800-THE LOST. It has trained 138,000 police and other professionals, disseminated more than 12 million free publications, and worked with law enforcement agencies on more than 50,000 missing child cases, resulting in the recovery of 32,000 children.

The fact that there have been 50,000 cases of missing children since 1984 may strike fear in the heart of every parent. So frequent are cases of missing children that a protocol has evolved: Posters are made, volunteers are recruited, a reward is offered and publicized, drawings are made if there is a suspect in the case. In 1973, no such protocols existed. We simply blundered our way through whatever things we could think of to assist the search, supported and helped by sympathetic and willing friends, neighbors, and organizations.

The National Center has distributed millions of photographs of missing children, and as a result one child in seven is recovered. The Center's literature says "NMEC believes that 'somebody knows', and seeks to reach every home in America." The center receives thousands of leads on missing children and forwards them to police investigators. It operates a national child pornography tipline in conjunction with the

U.S. Customs Service, the U.S. Postal Service, and the Federal Bureau of Investigation.

The Klaas Foundation for children of Sausalito, California, was founded by family and friends of the Klaas family after Polly Hannah Klaas was abducted from her home in Petaluma in 1993. The group which was to become the core of the Klaas foundation distributed two billion images of Polly worldwide during the 65-day search for the 12-year-old girl. The Klaas Foundation promotes nationwide parental awareness and child safety information, assists families of missing children, provides fingerprints and photo identification for children.

In 1996, Richard Allen Davis was convicted of kidnapping and murdering Polly and received the death sentence in California.

Since that time, the Klaas Foundation has been instrumental in lobbying for Megan's Law, which requires authorities to alert police and, in some cases, neighbors, when paroled sex offenders move into a community. The law takes its name from the case of Megan Kanka, who was seven years old when she was murdered in 1994 by a person with two previous convictions for molesting young girls.

Under Megan's law, a file was made public in July 1997, showing the names and addresses of persons convicted of molesting children. This file showed 57,000 registered "serious" sex offenders in California, 1,500 of them designated as "high-risk". There were four serious offenders registered as living in Moss Beach and seven serious offenders listed as living in Half Moon Bay.

In 1995, the NCMEC established its international division to handle international abductions and incoming international cases transferred from the State Department. On Jan. 26, 1990, the Hague Convention on the Civil Aspects of International Child Abduction was established to promote children's rights, making states that accept the convention accountable for their actions. Sixty-one countries signed the original agreement.

International child abduction is more than an occasional and incidental problem. In 1993, for instance, the United States Department of State worked on more than a thousand international child abduction cases.

In the past, foreign courts have often refused to recognize orders issued by courts in the United States. Since the Hague Convention treaty, a child who has been wrongfully removed or retained in a ratifying country must be returned to his or her country of habitual residence. The Convention also provides a means for helping parents to exercise visitation rights abroad.

Though custody cases are to be made in the abducted child's habitual residence, countries party to the Convention are expected to assist in the return of an internationally abducted child. More than 170 children have been returned since the establishment of the NCMEC International Division in September 1995.

The Hague Convention is a kind of children's bill of rights which includes political, economic, social and cultural human rights including the right to a name and nationality and protection from exploitation. The material in the Hague treaty was adapted from the United Nations Convention on the Rights of the Child, curiously not signed by the United States, though the US became a ratifying country of the Hague Convention in 1988.

It may be some consolation to the parents of missing children that these resources have been built on the grief and energy of survivors who were determined that the help they needed should be available to other children and families in distress.

NCMEC Age-Progression to 25   *NCMEC Age-Progression to 30*

NCMEC Age-Progression to 35   *Michaele's pencilled alterations*

CHAPTER NINETEEN:
SEARCHING FOR ANNA IN THE NINETIES

NATIONAL CENTER FOR MISSING AND EXPLOITED
CHILDREN
January 22, 1990
Dear Ms. Benedict:
Please forgive our delay in writing to tell you of the success of your direct mail letter. As of December 31, approximately 500 National Center donors mailed contributions totaling $9,577.31 in response to your touching letter.
This is a fantastic response. Once again, thanks so much for letting us use your letter to help the Center raise funds...
Hope all is well with you in California. Please let us know if you plan to visit the Washington, D.C. area any time this year. We would love to give you a tour of the Center and introduce you to our staff members.
Sincerely yours,
David L. Shapiro
Director of Education and Development

NATIONAL CENTER, September 25, 1992
On the occasion of Anna's birthday, our thoughts and prayers are with you. Keep hope alive. We are continuing to seek her safe recovery. Our most sincere wish is that next year you and Anna will celebrate her birthday together.
Your friends at the National Center

December 10, 1992

Ron Jones of the National Center called back and said he had spoken to Bill Cody at the San Mateo County Sheriff's Office. "He's working on your case," Ron said. I wanted to rule out any possible involvement by an Oakland man presently under suspicion in a child abduction case. Bill Cody telephoned various agencies including the Solano County police. He was familiar with the name and details of the suspect and the case. He called back later and said that the suspect in question was living and working in Maine from September 1972 to December 1973, according to the FBI.

If I had had Anna while I was married to Tony, she would have been named Antigone. The traditional system of names in Greece is that the first son is named for the paternal grandfather, as Nonda was named for Tony's father, Epaminondas. The second son is named for the maternal grandfather, as Ed was named for my father. The first daughter is named for the paternal grandmother, as the real Antigone Trimis, born in 1966 to Tony and his wife Elli, is named for Tony's mother, Antigone.

I didn't meet Antigone Trimis until she came to San Francisco in 1992, though Tony had sent photographs of her and her younger sister, Marina. Antigone had been in touch with her half-brothers, and I asked them if they thought I might meet her.

We sat in some park with my friend John and our friends Judy and Wylie. W. had been the Princeton English teacher at the Farm School in Greece the year after George was there. Antigone had dark hair, chopped off in a geometric cut. She had her father's hazel eyes. "You look like your Aunt Aphrodite," I said. "Everybody says that," she replied.

She had recently finished graduate school in drama at Brown University, and she had a job at the Magic Theater in San Francisco. Our birthdays were only four days apart. She wore glasses and played the piano and wore black tights. She didn't talk a lot, but when she did, it cut straight to the quick. "My God, she's smart", John and I told each other, several times.

Suddenly Nonda and Ed had a sister, one they had known about but not known. A real breathing person with her own history, some of which was connected indirectly to theirs and mine.

We hardly knew how to describe our relationship. Antigone would introduce me as her, ah, friend. Watching a play she'd directed, talking to her on the telephone, standing next to her at an Orthodox Easter service, I often thought of Antigone as my could-have-been daughter.

February 4, 1993

The mothers of three missing children confronted the suspect, Timothy Bindner, on the nationally syndicated Jane Whitney show.

Ann Campbell is the mother of Amanda (Nikki) Campbell, who disappeared at the age of seven from Fairfield, Calif., in December 1991. Kim Schwarz is the mother of Amber Schwarz-Garcia, who disappeared from Pinole in June 1988 at the age of seven. Sharon Nemeth is the mother of Michaela Garecht, who disappeared in October 1988, at the age of nine from Hayward.

Fairfield police detective Harold Sagan was quoted in the newspapers as saying "at the discretion of the district attorney's office, we have not arrested (Bindner)." Bindner's attorney, John Burris, has called the case a "failed investigation" that is now "being tried in the press."

I had a strange reaction to the television show, which seemed to have an extraordinary number of commercials, as well as credits for everybody's clothing and hairstyles. Somehow, I felt that the grief of these three mothers was being exploited for commercial purposes, and that the civil rights of the so-called suspect were in a precarious position, since he had not been officially accused of any crime. I wrote for a transcript of the program.

In the transcript, after "Theme music and applause", Whitney said "We've been hearing about a mother's anguish over her missing child. Joining us now by satellite is Tim Bindner, the man Ann (Campbell) says is responsible. Tim, you heard what she said during the last segment. What do you have to say to Ann Campbell?"

Bindner: " The first thing I'd like to say to her is that I didn't take your baby; I tried to find her as I've been doing on these horrifying cases here in the Bay Area ever since Amber disappeared back in 1988. All I did was to go out 11 days after Nikki disappeared and--conduct my own independent roadside search for one day along roads north of Fairfield. So she's--she's mistaken in thinking that I'm the person that did this. And I think that's probably because she's been talking to Harold Sagan and he's said he's convinced I did it."

December 8, 1993

A candlelight vigil has been scheduled for next Monday, and Coastsiders are invited to gather at the community tree on Main Street between the San Benito House and the Zabala House to remember Polly Klaas and other children who have been abducted. Polly was taken from her home two months ago and her body was found in a field last weekend. Richard Allen Davis has been charged with kidnapping and murder.

December 8, 1993

The Half Moon Bay Review has a story about Richard Davis, the suspect in the Polly Klaas murder case. He was born in San Francisco June 2, 1954 and went to Pescadero High School, but did not graduate. He pleaded guilty to breaking into a home when he was living in La Honda, at age 19, which puts him within less than ten miles of Purisima Canyon in 1973. He has an 11-page "rap sheet" of alleged crimes, including a conviction in 1985 for kidnapping a Redwood City woman at gunpoint from her apartment. He was sentenced to 16 years at Vacaville State Prison for this incident, and was paroled from Vacaville in June of this year.

December 10, 1993

Letter to the Editor, Coastside Journal

Almost 21 years ago, my daughter, Anna Christian Waters, disappeared from the back yard of our home on Purisima Creek Road, south of Half Moon Bay...the fact that Richard Allen Davis was living on the south coast at this time and that his connection with the death of a La Honda woman is being investigated again brings up the possibility that he may have been connected with other unexplained disappearances. I would like to know if he was connected with my daughter's disappearance...

However, I must take issue with some aspects of the response to the Polly Klaas kidnap/murder of which Davis is accused. We are surprised and shocked by violence, and yet we continue to condone and subsidize violence in the form of entertainment, lessons in martial arts, and easy access to lethal weapons. Stronger laws are being urged; the death penalty is being discussed again. Children are being enrolled in "self-defense" classes. Until we learn to recognize and resist violence at all levels and to practice peacefulness and forgiveness at all levels, we will continue to have victims. The perpetrator of violence is a victim, too.

Have You Seen Anna Waters?
By Bruce Davis, Journal News Editor

"Twenty-one years ago a mother listened to happy noises issuing from her back yard. She heard sounds--not words. Sounds that said her daughter, five-year-old Anna Christian Waters, played safely in their yard on rural Purisima Creek Road...."

The Coastside Journal, which was to last only a few more issues, used the age-advanced picture of Anna which the National Center had produced, reiterated many of the facts and speculations from the California Living article published almost 20 years previously.

April 12, 1994
Gordon McNeill was named head of the Federal Bureau of Investigation's newly-formed "crimes against children" task force in northern California. McNeill has led a two-month investigation into the kidnapping and slaying of Polly Klaas, and his current assignment includes a renewed attempt to solve eight kidnappings in the San Francisco Bay Area over the past decade.
The task force will employ new forensic technologies and computer systems to identify and track suspects. It is the first program of its kind in the country.
I wrote Mr. McNeill to make sure he knew that Anna's disappearance was still considered an open case in San Mateo County. He telephoned in response and said he was aware of the case. A nice man.

April 13, 1994
NATIONAL CENTER

In the 1990s, we have found that technological advances have helped to speed pictures and information about missing children to the public via computer, and state-of-the-art computer software has made it possible to age photographs of children who missing for two years or more. We have been incredibly fortunate to work with caring corporations who have brought these technological advances to our search for your children. We have another new program we would like you to participate in, which will further assist in these efforts.

We are in the process of building a video library of film footage of missing children, and would like to ask if you have home movies of your child which you would be willing to share with us. No matter what format it is in, we would like to request that you forward it to us so that we can use it in providing video to television stations nationwide who are interested in airing short segments on missing children. In cases where your child has been missing for more than two years, we will also provide those stations with a computer age progression of your child, if one has been completed.

Sincerely,
Ernie Allen, President

To Ben Ermini
Director of Case Management
NCMEC
April 22, 1994
    I received a letter from Ernie Allen today asking for home
movies of missing children, and I am sending you the only home
movie I have of my daughter, Anna Christian Waters. This film of a
camping trip was made in 1971 and Anna disappeared in January,
1973, so I do not know whether the movie is of any value. Anna is
the little blonde girl in the film; the two adults are her stepfather and
myself (divorced eight years ago); others are Anna's two brothers,
who were about nine and twelve, and a friend of the boys.

May 29, 1994
    Hatch Woods is now Purisima Creek Redwoods Open Space
Preserve. In 1996, San Mateo County joined Northwestern Santa
Clara County in creating the Midpeninsula Regional Open Space
District to which this park belongs. Although in the old days we
walked as far as the redwoods many times, I had not been in the park
until today, when I joined an herb walk led by a woman named
Suzanne E.
    A brochure on the park describes the woods which used to be
our back yard.
    "Located on the western slopes of the Santa Cruz Mountains
overlooking Half Moon Bay, this magnificent preserve, encompassing
2,519 acres, offers hikers, equestrians, and bicyclists a wide variety of
environments. The preserve was established with the donation of a
gift of two million dollars from Save the Redwoods League. Purisima
Creek Canyon provides towering redwoods and an understory of ferns,
berries and wildflowers.
    "Bordering the cool, moist canyon is Harkins Ridge with
coastal scrub to the north, and a hardwood forest of tan oak, madrone
and Douglas fir to the south. Thirteen miles of developed trails and
historical logging roads exist on the preserve. The two-mile Harkins
Fire Trail, accessible from the northerly parking area, connects the
parking area to Purisima Creek Road where visitors can ascend back to
Skyline Boulevard via the Whittemore Gulch Trail."
    Suzanne identified plants I had seen for years but knew little
about: The red elderberry, poisonous; the blue elderberry, useful for
making elderberry champagne; poison hemlock, related to Queen

Anne's lace but identifiable by the red striations on the stem; figwort, useful as a medication for skin diseases but contraindicated in heart disease; stachys bulata, also called horse mint or hedge nettle, a plant with cooling and calming qualities (I always called this "archangel".)

There were cleavers (gallium aperine), which stick to your clothing and which stimulate, Suzanne said, bile production. The garden pest, chickweed, grows near Purisima Creek and is used as a diuretic or for skin abrasions. Miner's lettuce (Montea perfoliata), from the purslane family, has properties similar to chickweed.

Periwinkle (vincia stipic major), though not native to the area, grows along the paths. The familiar stinging nettle (urtica holserida), full of formic acid, makes a healthful vegetable as well as good fertilizer when turned into tea. The shade-loving sweet cicily has seeds which aid digestion. We found all these and dozens more.

U. S. Department of Justice
Federal Bureau of Investigation
San Francisco
June 7, 1994

Dear Ms. Benedict,
This letter is to confirm the receipt of your letter of April 12, 1994. You can be assured that the case of Anna Christian Waters will be reviewed. I wish we could tell you that we can resolve this case but that might cause false hopes. You can be promised that your daughter will not be forgotten in our investigations and that the Task Force will be considering the applicability of developed information to your daughter's disappearance. Any new information will be shared with the San Mateo County Sheriff's Department immediately.

The Task Force prays that the knowledge of its awareness of your daughter will bring some comfort to yourself and your family. Special Agent J. Larry Taylor (phone) will be your contact. Please call him and provide your telephone number for future contacts.

Sincerely,
Jim R. Freeman
Special Agent in Charge
San Francisco FBI
(by SSA Gordon McNeill, Supervisor, Child Abduction Task Force)

NATIONAL CENTER
December 18, 1995

Dear Ms. Benedict,
        I am writing to let you know that your daughter's case is still
being monitored on a regular basis and that we will continue to do so
until she is found. The police also have the case listed as an open
investigation....we will continue to contact you regularly and please let
us know if we can provide any additional assistance in your search for
Anna.

Sincerely,
Ron Jones
Case Manager

March 9, 1996

Michaele:
        You have asked me one of the hardest questions there is. I
don't know what to say. I know many parents who have been
searching for their missing children for many years. They seem like
tortured souls to me. I guess the one advantage I have over any of
them, including you, is that I have closure.
        Look deep into your heart. Only there will you find your
answer. My heart bleeds for you. For 65 days I searched desperately
for my daughter (Polly Klass). I swore that I would never give up, but
who's to say how the years would have worn me down.

Marc Klaas

Letters to the Editor, San Francisco Chronicle, April 29, 1996

In Thursday morning's paper you mention several disappearances of children in the Bay Area, saying that Angela Bugay was the "first in a series"...My daughter, Anna Christian Waters, disappeared from our home in Half Moon Bay in 1973 at the age of five; the case has never been closed in San Mateo County, and while I know it has been a lifetime since her disappearance, I feel somehow compelled to let people know she was never accounted for and that her disappearance was never resolved.

Michaele Benedict

From Ed Trimis:

I wept. It had been many years since the disappearance of my sister but sometimes it still seemed to hurt like it was yesterday. ..I had a dream last night. It was about a little girl named Michelle who, in the dream, was my little girl who was missing. In the dream it was Michelle, but when I woke up I knew it was really Anna....

She was a beautiful little girl with wild and wavy blonde hair and a personality that wouldn't quit. When she was a baby, she would always say she had "natural curly hair" and...we would play along, teasing her, telling her that she curled her hair...

Most of the time I was fine. Even the little things that you might think would be upsetting, weren't. People asking "how many brothers and sisters do you have?" or seeing so many television specials or news reports about lost children. You know, they never made a movie about our family. Why is that? It seems that someone could have done something more...

I wish I could remember what I was doing when I heard the news. That's something people always say when major things happen in their lives. "I remember exactly what I was doing when President Kennedy was shot." When my sister disappeared, I don't remember.

From Nonda Trimis:

There is a Lost Bird Society which is named for a little girl who was orphaned in the Battle of Wounded Knee. Gary Stroutsos wrote a song called "Lost Bird". Didn't we sometimes call Anna Little Bird?

May 25, 1997

May 25 is now Missing Children's Day, and people who observe the day leave the porch light on, rather like the lantern in the window for the sailors far at sea.

CHAPTER TWENTY

No Stone Unturned

My sons' classmate at Half Moon Bay High School, Doug French, played Bellomy, the Girl's father, in a production of The Fantasticks put on at Half Moon Bay High School in 1974. I played piano; Nonda played drums, and Eddie played timpani. The boys stayed in touch with Doug through the years. I saw him at a reunion of the high school band in 2003 in Half Moon Bay.

I always loved Tom Jones and Harvey Schmidt's gently ironic song about children, which Doug sang and I played in the show.

Plant a radish, get a radish,
Never any doubt.
That's why I love vegetables.
You know what you're about…
They're dependable! They're
Befriendable!
They're the best friend a parent's
ever known!
While with children it's
bewilderin'
You don't know until the seed is
nearly grown

Doug, The Fantasticks, 1974   Just what you've sown…

("The Fantasticks" by Harvey Schmidt and Tom Jones, 1960, copyright Music Theater International, New York, N. Y.)

In summer of 2005, I had a call from Doug, who tactfully sounded me out on the matter of looking for Anna, using tactics which were not available before days of the Internet. This is Doug's story:

in·jus·tice

NOUN:
1. Violation of another's rights or of what is right; lack of justice.
2. A specific unjust act; a wrong.

From   The American Heritage[R] *Dictionary of the English Language:*
Fourth Edition. 2000.

"Injustice anywhere is a threat to justice everywhere"
-Martin Luther King, Jr.

By any definition, the events of January 16th, 1973 were an injustice. Bad things happened to good people without justification or reason. A young girl was removed from her adoring family and a mother was deprived of seeing her daughter grow into womanhood. And the injustice continues every day that the family is denied knowing what happened to Anna.

I met Anna's family one year after her disappearance. My family moved to Half Moon Bay in January 1974 from Sacramento, California. Half Moon Bay is a beautiful place with gorgeous weather – about five days out of the year. Unfortunately, the other 360 days, it is cold, wet, foggy and generally miserable. The weather matched my enthusiasm for leaving my friends in Sacramento and making this unwanted move.

It was in the middle of this foggy time that I first set foot on the HMB High School campus and went to the office to check in for my first day of school. After completing the necessary registration paperwork, the school secretary asked a passing student to show me the way to my first class. This student was Nonda Trimis, Anna's older brother.

Nonda was a sophomore like myself and we shared an interest in both music and fishing. He was an accomplished drummer and suggested that I join the school band. My musical experience up to that point had been playing the guitar with a lack of skill that made Danny Partridge look like Jimmy Hendrix.

Later, when Nonda had invited me over to his house, I met his brother Ed. Ed was a piano virtuoso and a chess master. Many days would soon be wasted in intense chess battles signifying nothing other than bragging rights to being king of the board. Ed also played the bagpipes – an instrument that curiously can be one of great emotional content or one that sounds like someone ran over a cat's tail.

Joe Ford, the boys' stepfather, was a charismatic chap with a leather riverboat gambler's hat, an ever present smile and a twinkle in his eyes. Joe would join us boys in impromptu touch football games or on our frequent fishing trips on the rocky Montara shoreline. Joe was, in the language of a teenager of the time, a "cool parent". I envied Nonda and Ed.

The matriarch of the family was Mikie. Dressed in typical hippie garb, she would provide her boys (and often me in tow) with hot meals and a warm home. Her talents on piano provided a foundation on which her boys could later expand on to create divergent careers in music of their own. Her love of her family would teach her sons how to provide the love required for them to be the fathers that they would become.

But something was missing. As happy as the family was, there was an underlying sadness that would surface at times that was hard to understand from the outside. A conversation over dinner, something said that brought back unwanted emotions, a painful recognition by all who knew the story, and a quick change of topic to preserve the genial times.

I do not recall when I first learned of Anna and her disappearance. It must have been shortly after my meeting the family. Her disappearance was big news in a town where the second biggest story was when someone's pet monkey escaped and was seen swinging from the trees. No one ever hid the fact, it was more a situation of how does one introduce such a painful subject into light-hearted conversation? I do know that I was both fascinated and horrified with the injustice of it all.

The fight against injustice has always been a quest of mine. I remember when I was in second grade, I attended a school where a whistle was blown during lunchtime to mark when we could start eating (not unlike how meals are regulated at maximum security prisons). One time, when the whistle was blown, a kid sitting across from me screamed at the top of his lungs for no other reason than he thought it was funny. The teacher with the whistle immediately ran to our table and apprehended who she thought was the culprit...me! I protested as much as I could as I was dragged to the principal's office, but to no avail. I sat in a detention room for the rest of the day and my parents were notified of my egregious and felonious ways. That day I vowed that I would always fight injustice – especially when I was the victim!

However, the vows of righteous anger of a child are often dulled by the monotonous grind of daily adulthood. We often lose connection to those principles that formed who were as we march through the years toward who have become. It is easy to compromise our beliefs and, ultimately, ourselves.

As the years passed by, we all went our separate ways. Nonda became a professional musician, a carpenter and then an architect. Ed became a music teacher, eventually moving into administration at inner-city public schools in Los Angeles. Joe and Mikie divorced, with Joe moving to the East Coast and Mikie eventually remarrying a charming cello player named Charles.

But there always was the question of Anna.

When I first learned of the story of Sharon Marshall, my first thought was of Anna. The tale of Sharon Marshall is one of the saddest ones that I have ever heard. Sharon was a child who was raised by a non-related pedophile from about age five. When Sharon grew to adulthood, the pedophile married her and turned her to a life of stripping and prostitution. Sharon eventually tried to break free from her tormenter and was killed in a mysterious hit-and-run accident. She died without the world ever knowing her true name and how she had come to be under the influence of a monster.

My knowledge of the Sharon Marshall case was limited to what information had been presented on a television episode of "Unsolved Mysteries". At this time, my knowledge of Anna's case was even less – it resided in clouded memories of long-forgotten conversations about a subject that no one wanted to recall. I was able to discover that Sharon's history had been traced back to 1975 and that Anna had disappeared in 1973. Both girls were blonde and had a superficial resemblance to each other. I thought that I may have stumbled on to the answer to two mysteries at once.

I searched the Internet for information about both cases. I discovered that a book named "A Beautiful Child" by Matt Birkbeck (Berkley Publishing Company, New York, 2004) was the ultimate resource on information about Sharon. I also scoured the various missing person's websites for details about Anna. I discovered that Sharon's abductor, Franklin Delano Floyd, had been released from prison in January 1973 (the earliest possible time of when he could have "obtained" Sharon). I also found that Anna had disappeared January 16, 1973. I also found that Anna, along with several other missing girls from the same era, was being considered as a potential match for Sharon. I found nothing in either story that could rule out a possible match.

I agonized over my next step. I believed that enough information existed to warrant further investigation, but that would require involvement by Anna's family – and I surely did not want to reopen old wounds that time, if not healed, at least allowed the pain to go numb so that the family could continue on. Bringing back that pain, without providing an answer to their questions, was the last thing I wanted to do.

I worried, I prayed, I worried some more, then I dialed Mikie's phone number. Mikie answered and was patient as I probed around the issue to see if she was willing to entertain another run at solving Anna's disappearance. She was not aware of the Sharon Marshall case. I suggested that she purchase Matt Birkbeck's book – warning her that it was brutally honest in listing the horrors that Sharon endured. I asked her to see if anything in it rang a bell as far as relating to Anna.

A few days later, Mikie called and let me know that she did not believe that Sharon and Anna were the same person. Anna has brown eyes, where Sharon's were blue. Also, most importantly, she did not believe that Sharon resembled Anna.

I then faced a choice: Do I say, "Sorry to have bothered you", hang up and forget all about Anna's disappearance, or do I decide to continue the search to its final conclusion? As a man in his late forties, I am at an age when we start to contemplate our place in the cosmos. Some buy a Corvette and run off with their secretary. Some sigh a surrender to meaninglessness and continue to plug along as they have done every day of their life. I decided that until I discover a cure for cancer, this was going to be my contribution to righteousness in the world.

I asked Mikie if I could look into Anna's case further. She said "Yes."

Little did I know how this conversation would change my life and the lives of people who I had yet to meet.

Websleuths.com

One of the first orders of business was to inventory what strengths and weaknesses I was bringing to the search for Anna. I always have had an overabundance of confidence in my own abilities to do…just about everything. (My wife has always said that I am my own biggest fan.) I had spent years coaching college level speech and debate and felt that I possessed the ability to logically examine any situation or evidence that I discovered. But I quickly realized that I had absolutely zero experience in investigating a missing person case.

Fortunately, while I had been researching the Sharon Marshall case, I had discovered a website called "Websleuths.com", an online crime-fighting community for people who had exactly the talents that I lacked. I originally posted information about Anna in the Sharon Marshall forum, but then started a forum dedicated exclusively to Anna when the investigation led us away from any relationship to Sharon.

People began to pay attention to our efforts and many more people joined the search. One thing that separated Anna's forum from many of the others on Websleuths.com (WS) was that Anna's family members were able to provide first-hand information and answers to the investigator's questions. Mikie joined the forum as "Annasmom". Nonda participated as "Annasbro". I also located Joe Ford (whose previous investigations had provided the foundation of our soon to be made advances) who contributed to the forum under his name "Joe Ford".

One of the greatest strengths of a community effort such as WS is the wealth of knowledge that vast numbers of investigators bring to the search. Some of the researchers are active and retired law enforcement. Some bring genealogical research skills. Others are experts at locating people who do not necessarily want to be found. No matter what question has arisen on some obscure topic, someone in the WS community has direct and expert knowledge about the subject. The sum is so much greater than the individual parts.

Many talented people have contributed to the search. But one treasure that we have found is a poster who goes by the name of "SherlockJr", Maureen Wyenandt. She has brought to the search a tenacity and vigor that has sustained us when our own determination has wavered. Her abilities as a researcher are unparalleled and she has joined the family circle as a trusted and valued member. Many of the advances that we have made are because of her contributions.

And we have made advances that move us incrementally closer to finding Anna.

The Name Eifee

When I first started investigating this case, it dawned on me that if Anna was taken by her birth father, there might be a paper trail created in the seventies and eighties that no one knew would be accessible in the new century with the Internet (much as cold cases are now being solved with DNA tests that were not in existence during the commission of crimes).

Working on the hypothesis that Anna may have been taken by George Waters and hidden until he was no longer a suspect, I realized that it was possible that she could have been raised under her actual name as compared to an alias. Michaele informed me that Anna actually had two separate birth certificates - one as Anna Christian Waters and one with the added middle name of "Eifee". "Eifee" is a nonsense word that the father's "mentor" insisted be added to her name for "numerological" reasons.

I did a Google search for the word 'Eifee' and received about 150 matches. Virtually all of the hits were from foreign language web sites except for a handful. Among those in English, only one site showed that someone was using 'Eifee' as a login name. I examined the member profiles from this forum and discovered that the person who was using 'Eifee" as a login was actually named Anna. This was either a tremendous breakthrough or an extremely cruel coincidence.

I tried to send an e-mail to the address, but it was returned as a closed account. This is not uncommon - most free e-mail sites will automatically close after a certain period of inactivity. I joined the provider myself to see what information they would have had to received to open an account. An applicant would have had to provide a first and last name, a birth date and the zip code of their residence. If we could uncover this information and they matched up with Anna's particulars, then we would perhaps have found Anna. Several members of Websleuths.com joined in the hunt for Eifee.

I later discovered that all of our research on this email address had been based on a mistake: there was an underscore in the address that was not identifiable when viewing the address. A new contact email was sent to the correct address.

I finally heard back from the elusive "Eifee". She was a young Asian woman in her twenties living in New Zealand. She had used the name "Eifee" because it was her favorite character from the Pokemon card series – a fact that was news to us! Her actual name was Joanna, not Anna – she had used the alias of "Anna" in an effort to maintain a level of privacy on her web posts. Ironically, it was this attempt at privacy that ultimately lead to dozens of researchers discovering every little detail about her life. Ah, the law of unintended consequences...

Attention then shifted to the origin of the actual word "Eifee". Since Pokemon was not created until decades after Anna had been given the name, it became obvious that this was nothing more than an unfortunate coincidence. However, Brody had to have had some basis for creating this particular name. We set out to find it.

One of the researchers discovered that "EEFIE" (Eifee spelled backwards) was the name of an organization of medical students in Greece. George Waters had studied medicine in Greece, so this looked very promising. However, further research uncovered that the organization was founded in the 1990's, years after Waters had died, so this was not the source of the mysterious name.

Another researcher pointed out that the name "Effie" was a somewhat common name in the late 1800's and early 1900's. Very few were being given that name in the 1960's. It is possible that "Eifee" was a bastardized spelling of "Effie".

Forum members began to research numerology and the reasons behind George Brody's and George Waters' insistence that Anna's name be changed so that it would reflect a numerological value of 27 like that of Brody, or so he said.

One member, searching for the name Eifee, came across a reference to a religious sect founded in Vancouver in the 1930s: Kabalarians. The central belief, this member wrote, has to do with numerology, or a belief in the mystical powers of numbers. Because of this, he said, many members of the cult change their names to those which they think will have greater value.

Michaele visited the website and stated that the beliefs of the Kabalarians were very reminiscent of Brody's diatribes. The Kabalarians maintained a church in the San Francisco Bay Area in the 1960's, but no evidence has been located to link Brody directly to the Kabalarians.

Since the two Georges had insisted that Anna's name include the name "Eifee", it continues to remain a focal point of our research. If they were involved in her disappearance, the name "Eifee" may still be part of Anna's identity.

Playing Hide and Seek with Anna

When planning out how to organize the search for Anna, I envisioned a two- prong approach. First, we would find out all we could concerning Anna's disappearance and follow the leads until we found her. The other approach was to try and see if she was out there looking for her family. The most likely scenario is that Anna was told that she was adopted – if so, then she may very well have been posting on various adoption reunion websites searching for her birth parents. This duet of strategies turned up many promising leads.

I found a profile on a website of an Anna Waters in a southern state whose age was listed as 37. The eyes and hair color match, but the picture was too washed out to look for a mole or dimples. The face was much thinner and the chin was much more angular compared to the age progressions of Anna, but enough is similar to ask Michaele her opinion. She saw several family traits in the photograph and stated that it was worthy of further investigation.

Contacting this Anna proved to be more difficult than I had bargained for. I could not locate an address or phone number for her. When she did not return my emails, I called every Waters in the town where she lived, spoke to fourteen people, and ascertained that they did not know the Anna. It is always possible that someone was covering for her, assuming that I was a bill collector or a stalker.

Eventually (perhaps after she had been contacted by her family members about the weird Yankee stalker), she responded to my inquiries and assured me that she knew her parentage and origins.

While searching websites dedicated to reuniting adoptees and their birth families, I discovered a young woman named Susan who was born in San Francisco on September 25, 1967 (the same date and location as Anna) and was seeking her parents. Her vital statistics all matched with Anna: Caucasian, brown hair and eyes. She had listed contact information that was current when she posted it, but was out-of-date five years later when I tried to contact her. The hunt was on…

I did statistical research into the number of Caucasian girls born during an average day in San Francisco during 1967 to determine what the odds were of this woman being Anna. Demographic breakdowns for the year of 1967 showed that on average, five Caucasian females would have been born. For the adopted girl not to be Anna would mean that out of that five, one girl was adopted and one girl was abducted--pretty thin odds that these two events would occur in such a small sampling. I personally put the odds of this being Anna at 50/50 (and I may have been conservative). I quickly found out that I am no mathematician.

Eventually, I was able to locate updated contact information on a high school reunion site. I sent a new email to her current address and then…nothing. Posters on the Websleuths.com site were naturally anxious to hear if we had finally located Anna. I contacted the adoptee's high school in an attempt to get her transcripts and yearbook picture to compare to pictures of Anna, but the transcripts would require a court order and the yearbooks would require a trip to her hometown library (about three hours away).

Three hours later, I was at the library and viewing high school pictures of a girl who could be Anna. I viewed the adoptee's yearbook photos and the conclusion was…inconclusive. I was hoping for either a clear match or an obvious no-match. Instead, what I found was a girl whose hair seemed darker than I was expecting, with a more angular face and a nose that came to a sharper point than any of Anna's pictures. However, she definitely had pronounced dimples like Anna's and nothing in the picture ruled her out. I was only able to find pictures of her for her freshman and sophomore year.

On Jan. 16, the 33rd anniversary of Anna's disappearance, I received a phone call from the adoptee. That day I posted the following message on WS: "I have spoken to the adoptee and she is not Anna. The adoptee was adopted at age five weeks and based on that has no memories of her birth family. Anna was abducted at age five years and would have some memories, however vague. The adoptee has adoption papers from a legitimate private agency (one that has been around for more than a century), so in the absence of any falsified paperwork, there is no reason to believe that she is Anna. "Thanks to all of you for your hopes and prayers. I believe that Anna is still out there...We search on."

One positive of the research into this adoptee was that I was able to provide her with a list of every girl born in San Francisco on September 25, 1967. I also was able to rule out about half of the names on that list since I was able to trace those girls' history into adulthood. That left her with a handful of names to research as possibly being her birth-name.

Maureen Wyenandt, known as SherlockJr on Websleuths.com, has had amazing success at locating a series of adoptees whose histories indicate that they could be Anna. Her stories and a letter from one of the adoptees follow in Chapter 21.

Maureen's tireless work on the behalf of Anna and the adoptees has resulted in numerous reunions. We pray that her efforts will lead to one more - a reunion for Anna.

The Couple in the Car

Nonda provided what is probably the single biggest clue in answering what may have happened to Anna: He recalled that he and Ed had witnessed an attempt by a couple in a car to lure Anna into the vehicle about one month before she actually disappeared.

Nonda posted the following on the Websleuths.com forum:

"As far as I remember it, here is the accounting of the incident with the car luring Anna towards it: It seemed like the middle of the day. Maybe it was a Saturday or Sunday. We used to like to walk towards the end of the canyon down the road heading east. The house where we lived was about 1.5 miles from the end of the canyon. We were approximately 1/4 mile from our house when a car passed us and pulled in front of us about 25 ft. Saturn the dog barked at the car as a woman wearing a loose fitting white shirt with embroidery on it and

long dark hair opened up the back door. She spoke to us from within the car, a 4 door American sedan that was a dark green or gold. Somehow I remember it as a Chevy Impala late 60s - it was not new. I know cars pretty well. I thought it had the old style Washington plate - white with green letters - I can't be sure about that

"When we got the dog settled down she made small talk and addressed Anna primarily - I believe. I answered for her but she continued to address Anna with small talk and questions - do you live here? Where do you go to school? Do you walk down the road often? At that point she asked if she wanted her (us - I can't remember) to ride to the end of the road with her. This creeped me out sufficiently to turn our party around and head back home. The woman closed the door and the car scooted off quickly towards the end of the canyon. I don't remember if and how I relayed the story at the time to my parents.

"I didn't think much of it. I knew some creepy people would travel down that road every once in a while. A body was dumped closer to the entry of the canyon earlier that year. I just knew there was no way any of us was going to get into a car with people we didn't know and kind of put it behind me. I wish now I had played closer attention to everything.

"Being so long ago it is a bit fuzzy. She was in the front seat. There was a driver. She or someone in the back (they might have stayed in the car) opened the back door. She approached us. She was early to mid 30s I would guess. She had long straight black hair and a loose fitting cotton blouse with embroidery on it like a Mexican or Indian type blouse. I don't remember her having any accent just that she was overly friendly in a weird way for someone we didn't know."

The significance of this event cannot be overstated. This means that one month before Anna disappeared, a couple attempted to get Anna to get in their car. It would be reasonable to assume that they returned at the later time and successfully abducted Anna. This scenario raises the possibility that Anna was taken by a family that would raise her as their daughter. And that she could be alive today, looking for her real family.

A Plan for Abduction?

When George Waters committed suicide, his personal papers were collected by his brother Bill who forwarded them on to Michaele to assist in the search for Anna. When I became involved, she gladly passed the materials to me in the form of what has become known as the "Box from Hell". It contained all of Waters' documentation from 1966 until his death in 1982 – banking receipts, personal correspondence, and legal paperwork involved in his draft status, etc.

Suspiciously, there is a lack of material from the time period right around when Anna disappeared. Michaele suspected that Waters had spent the period between the death of Brody and his own death purging his files of anything that might relate to Anna.

However, recently, a single sheet of paper was discovered that potentially shows that Waters and Brody did in fact have a hand in the disappearance. A handwritten note was found that said the following:

Plan

1. Contact ~~m~~ont p̄ final arrangement c̄ c's have been made. (Jan. 1973)

2. Apply for $100,000 c̄ A&E, as ~~Beneficiary~~

3. 3 months later, negotiate increase to 5. s4/4 c̄ A&E.

4. 3 mos later change B.

Translated, the note says:

Plan

1. Contact MONY with Final arrangements with L's have been made. (Jan. 1973)
2. Apply for $100,000 with A.C.E. (Anna Christian Eifee) as B.[eneficiary – scribbled over]
3. 3 months later, negotiate increase to 5[00,000] still with A.C.E.
4. 3 months later, change B.[eneficiary]

This note means that something requiring advanced planning was to occur involving Anna in January 1973 involving insurance policies. Waters had already taken out numerous accidental death policies on himself with Brody as the beneficiary prior to the writing of this note. None of these other policies required "final arrangements" or the changing of the beneficiary – they just required the filling out of paperwork and the payment of a premium. Something was different about this transaction, and it involved Anna.

Could this be the missing link to tie Waters and Brody to Anna's disappearance? Could one of the motivations behind the abduction be that it was part of an insurance scheme that required Anna to disappear for policies to be changed over to Brody as the beneficiary?

One question that remains unanswered is the reference "L's". Waters did have an insurance policy issued by Lloyd's of London. Another possible meaning is "Lawyers". Or perhaps, "L's" is the initial for the couple in the car who had been seen attempting to lure Anna in to their vehicle and may have returned to complete the deed.

Whatever the exact meaning of each word in the note is, it does seem to confirm that Waters and Brody were involved in a plan centering around Anna that would allow them to change beneficiaries after an event that would occur in January 1973. Anna disappeared in January 1973, creating a situation that allowed them to change the beneficiary from Anna to Brody. Maybe Brody had the psychic abilities that he claimed and he was able to view into the future, or he was a conman who manipulated people and events to culminate in Anna's disappearance. I choose to believe the latter.

Later discoveries in the Box from Hell confirmed that this "plan" had been in place for several years at least. Brody was obviously concerned that Anna represented an obstacle to him receiving any insurance settlements or inheritance from Waters. Waters dutifully followed each and every one of Brody's demands. Waters drew up a will listing Brody as his heir, willing only a single dollar to Anna in an effort to demonstrate that this was his specific decision and not an oversight on his part. Waters requested that if he were to die while overseas, the U.S. State Department only notify Brody – not Waters' family. Waters' insurance policies all included a picture of Brody with the request that only the man depicted in the picture be paid any benefits – this would allow Brody to collect without presenting any other identification. Every move was done to protect Brody's interests and to block Anna's interests as Waters' only legal heir.

Brody and Waters were obsessed with making sure that Anna would not interfere with Brody becoming rich at the death of Waters. Anna's disappearance insured this result. This is either coincidence or, as I believe, evidence of motive.

Margaret Kukoda

Margaret Kukoda was the woman that George Brody lived with prior to his living with George Waters. Margaret developed cancer and was treated by Waters. It was during this period that Waters met Brody who was a frequent visitor of Kukoda in the hospital. Margaret passed away August 3, 1967 (her 50th birthday).

We have been able to trace that Margaret and Brody lived together since before 1962 at a residence on Noe Street in San Francisco. We have not been able to follow their connection farther back than that, but it appears that they both were from Pennsylvania, so it is possible that they knew each other prior to Margaret moving to San Francisco (circa 1943), when she started work as a nurse at a military hospital in the Bay Area.

Margaret left the Navy in 1951. In 1952, she plead guilty and was placed on four months probation for performing illegal abortions at her residence (she admitted to four such abortions). As a result of her conviction, she lost her nursing license and began working at various businesses in the Bay Area. She worked under the names Margaret Kukoda, Mary Kukoda and Mary Kay (she may have sold Mary Kay cosmetics for a while).

The nature of the relationship between Margaret and Brody is unknown, other than it was close enough that they resided together and that Brody had power of attorney during her final illness.

Our initial interest in Margaret was only to understand her relationship with Brody. Margaret passed away 1-1/2 months before Anna was born and 5-1/2 years before Anna disappeared – she had absolutely zero involvement in her disappearance and was probably a victim of Brody's delusions of grandeur also. However, due to the fact that Brody believed that Anna was the reincarnation of Margaret, the possibility that Anna had been taken by the two Georges and placed with an unwitting family member of Margaret was something that deserved examination.

We discovered that a female Kukoda that was approximately the same age as Anna had moved from New York to San Francisco in the 1990's, even living within five miles of Michaele's home in Montara for a time. This Kukoda enjoyed the hobby of long distance running, the same as Anna's brother Nonda (a shared genetic trait?). More to the point, this was the only Kukoda to move to California since Margaret in 1943. Could it be that she was drawn to the area by memories of a life there before?

Researchers were able to identify that K. Kukoda had married and moved to another Northern California town using her new married name. We were able to locate her new address and phone number. I called her and tried to gently prod her to answer some questions. Her response was, shall we say, brusque. She stated that she had never heard of Margaret Kukoda and was not related to her, and that she was too busy to speak any more. Thus ended our conversation, but not the search.

Law enforcement, at our request, obtained the DMV photograph of K. Kukoda and compared it to the age-progressed pictures generated by the NCMEC. It was the unanimous opinion of the detectives that reviewed the photographs that this Kukoda was not Anna.

Eventually, we were able to make contact with part of Margaret's family living on the East Coast. They were extremely helpful and gracious in providing information. They contacted Margaret's one surviving sibling who gave us details of Margaret's move to California during World War II. She had been accompanied by her boyfriend named "Russell". Could Russell have been Brody? We quickly emailed pictures of Brody to the family to see if he and Russell were the same person. The sibling said that the picture of Brody was not the same man as Russell.

The openness and kindness of the Kukoda family in assisting with this portion of mystery has convinced us that there is absolutely no possibility of them having any connection, even unwittingly, to Anna's disappearance. They too were victims, albeit distant, of the con man Brody.

The Mysterious Mr. Brody

George Brody was an odd little man whose life was wrapped in a mystery of his own design. He fancied himself to be an aristocrat, a genius, even a messiah. What he really was is an egotistical delusional con man who preyed upon the sickness of George Waters. At a time when Waters needed medical care for his schizophrenia, instead he got Brody.

The more I look into this case, the more that I am convinced that George Brody is the "Rosetta Stone" that will unlock answers to Anna's disappearance. If he and George Waters were not involved, it would be such a strange set of coincidences: that Michaele would lose her husband to an odd con-man AND lose her daughter to a stranger abduction within a five year period. No, common sense tells me that the two events were related.

My discussions with Joe Ford have reinforced the level of paranoia that the two Georges lived every day of their later years with. They would not even step out of their hotel room without immediately beginning "evasive" maneuvers to avoid being followed (doubling back without warning, making numerous turns in direction for no reason, etc.) What is humorous in a twisted sort of way is that they were being followed (The old joke: Just because you're paranoid doesn't mean you aren't being watched). They also used several aliases in their day-to-day business (Brody was also known as "George Bee", while Waters was registered at the hotel as "Walters".)

Joe Ford posted the following information:

"In the summer of 1973, when the ranch and the creek had been scoured for the 30th time, when the scouts and the searchers no longer returned, when the hue and cry was no longer loud and the story less newsworthy and the Sheriff's Department had turned its attention to more solvable crimes and were now reluctant to return our calls, we decided it was now up to us, alone, to find Anna.

The investigation of Anna's father by the county detectives seemed cursory and inconclusive and promptly abandoned. We decided to find out for ourselves what, if anything, GW (Anna's father) knew of Anna's whereabouts.

We discovered that Waters was working the evening shift at a local San Francisco hospital. After several attempts I managed to follow him by car to a shabby semi-transient hotel in the Tenderloin District of San Francisco. I was aware from stories told by Michaele of the strange behavior and paranoia exhibited by Brody and Waters so was not surprised by their choice of residence. Complete anonymity.

I returned the following day with rented cameras and equipment. Parked across the street with the windows to our old VW van obscured with taped-on garbage bags, I had a good view of the hotel entrance. I was lucky enough to get a few pictures of them exiting the hotel...

After several, mostly futile, attempts at following them by vehicle through the illusive streets of SF and to myriad restaurants and cafes, two things became apparent. They were exceedingly weird and exceptionally paranoid. But did they have a connection to Anna's disappearance? I needed to somehow get closer.

I first rented a room in the equally shabby hotel next to theirs. The room was located on the same level and adjacent to theirs, separated by a service alley. I was in a position to see directly into their room. Unfortunately they kept the blinds down to within six inches of the sill the whole time. It was no problem, however, to ascertain that they lived alone in the room - with no signs of a child or any visitor for that matter. I observed and followed them for the next few days, learning nothing more.

Over a period of time I eventually acquired a room in the same hotel and on the same floor as Brody and Waters. With a wild and unlikely tale to the hotel proprietors, I was able to rent the room next to theirs when it became available. I listened and observed.

I can no longer be sure how many hours, days and nights I spent following their erratic footsteps and listening to their strange dialogues. I know that I taped over forty hours of numbing drivel in the hopes of capturing a clue to Anna's disappearance. I believe I had several seemingly relevant tapes transcribed.

Brody and Waters, albeit bizarre, did have a routine and daily schedule. Weekdays would find GW hurrying off early to one or another of his jobs. Respectably dressed but with an air of preoccupation. His work leaned toward nonpersonal interaction e.g. an outpatient alcoholic clinic and a walk-in non-emergency clinic. Brody would slip out of the hotel early morning as well and could be found monopolizing a weary waitress with breakfast at a downtown eatery. A brisk walk back to the hotel and he was in for the day- amusing himself with TV, newspaper and his own running commentary. The telephone would ring several times a day. Waters checking-in for advice and/or instructions. Dry cleaning and the like. Always hush-hush, as though these were topics of great import. "Now repeat that back to me."

Nights were a different matter entirely. Brody seemed to come alive with the night. Somehow energized. Waters would usually arrive at the hotel around 7:00 or 8:00 pm, having showered at work no doubt. [The rooms at the hotel contained a bed, a facsimile of a dresser, a table, chair and sink. There was a bathroom down the hall avoided by all but the seriously deranged.] Their nights were spent scurrying from one dreary diner to the next interspersed with return trips to the hotel where Brody would harangue Waters to remember every word of every conversation with every waitress that misguidedly spoke to them. Brody was consummately self-centered and imagined himself the Lothario of S.F. and heartthrob to every poor waitress that they met. The encounters had to be repeated over and over again until every ounce of self-aggrandizement was squeezed from them.

Poor Waters. I felt sorry for him. This was a typical scene, one to be repeated night after night. He hardly ever got more than two or three hours sleep. There is no doubt in my mind that sleep deprivation played a large part in the control exerted by Brody over Waters consciously or not.

In short order the surveillance began to take its toll on me as well. I worked as a carpenter and house builder by day and inhabited this Runyonesque stage at night, surrounded by hookers and pimps and cagey street hustlers, thugs and thuggers, mugs and muggers. The S.F. Tenderloin is no place for the faint-hearted. I felt myself becoming seduced by its intrigue and unhealthy energy.

I decided it was time to provoke a response from the two. I penned a letter to Waters pleading with him to respond if he had any knowledge of Anna's whereabouts or was interested in the search. I mailed it to his work address and waited by the recorder for three days until it was delivered. As expected, Waters came directly to the hotel and showed it to Brody. There was a silence deep with tension as I strained to hear. "I'm glad the tot is dead," Waters mumbled. Brody was, for once, at a loss for words. The subject was changed. Anna's name was not mentioned then or thereafter. My letter was discovered upon Water's death, unopened and torn in two.

Disappointed and weary, I abandoned my surveillance of this sad yet pitiful duo. It seemed to me that their involvement in Anna's disappearance was unlikely despite their odd behavior.

I can not say for certain that Brody and Waters were innocent of Anna's abduction if such it was. Better and more resourceful minds than mine may yet discover their involvement. As for me, I remain clueless in this sorrowful search for that elusive key that will unlock the mystery of a child that was here one moment and gone the next."

The forum began to look for information on Brody and came up with some odd facts: One George Brody, born Feb. 18, 1920, in New York, N. Y., died July 17, 2002, and was buried in B'nai Jacob Cemetery in Pueblo Chieftain, Colorado. Another forum member found a George Brody on the 1930 Federal Census, born in 1919, son of Sigmund and Sarah Brody, living in Boston, Massachusetts, at the time of the census. She found another George Brody born "about 1923" living in Salt Lake City during the 1930 census. Another George Brody, son of Samuel and Rebecca Brody, was born "about 1923" and was living in Wilkes-Barre, Lucerna County, Pennsylvania, during the same census. Another forum member found a George Brody with a birth date of "about 1896", an immigrant from Czechoslovakia in 1913. He was living in a Chicago boarding house in 1930, with his occupation listed as "laborer".

An inquiry by the San Francisco Public Administrators office listed Brody's birth date as August 15, 1923, in Massachusetts. No relatives were ever discovered.

Any of the above details are highly suspect because the 'facts' most likely came from George Waters who, along with Brody, went to great lengths to hide information about themselves.

I had an epiphany about George Brody: A birth year of 1923 would have made him only 58 years old when he died. Joe Ford took a picture of Brody in 1974, when he would have been 51 years old according to this birth date. This is not the picture of a man in his early fifties. So the birth date of 1923 is surely false. I would guess that he was born somewhere in the range of 1895 through 1910.

We continue to peel away the layers of the onion known as George Brody. Eventually, the truth of who he was will be exposed.

Spreading The Word

When I first began to investigate the story of Anna, there were few references to her on the Internet. Among those few references, several were incorrect or incomplete. Past history has shown us that incorrect information will lead people to incorrect conclusions, so we set out to update and correct any mentions of Anna. The operators of those sites have been gracious and eager to provide the corrected information.

We also set out to increase the "web presence" of Anna's story. Because of the fractured nature of the Internet, it is important that the word of Anna's disappearance be published in many places – the more, the better. This increases the chances that the right person with the right missing clue will see that her family is continuing to search for her.

The members of Websleuths.com have stepped up to the challenge by creating informational sites in several places. Several have started MySpace pages about Anna. There also is a MySpace page created to help identify Brody. Other sites have been created by members throughout cyberspace. Members have also been instrumental in locating sites that have incorrect information and bringing them to our attention.

Because of the viral nature of the Internet, increased web presence leads to additional web presence. Several sites have included Anna's story among the information that they provide – sites owned by people that we have never met, yet they have adopted our search as their own.

On January 16th, 2007, I appeared on the Internet radio show "Missing Pieces", hosted by Todd Matthews. Todd is famous among amateur sleuthers for his success in solving the "Tent Girl" case. He dedicated over an hour to the history and current status of our search for Anna. This brought even more people to the Websleuths.com site and increased public awareness.

Each new venue to tell Anna's story has helped bring us closer to an answer.

(Note from Mikie): *On September 20, 2006, Marc Longpre at the Half Moon Bay Review wrote a story about the search for Anna, correcting misconceptions from the original Review story of 1973 and including pictures of "The Plan", the kindergarten and age-advanced pictures of Anna and a photo of Doug and Mikie distributing flyers along Purisima Creek Road. One of the flyers went to the mailbox of the farm from which Anna disappeared.*

We had previously sent letters to the owner of the farm, a well-known singer and songwriter whose home studio may well have been the barn where Anna sometimes played. We never had any response, though the lyrics to one of the woman's songs were curiously resonant with our search:

Bad girls run fast

Leave home alone

No trace or clue of where they've gone

Sometimes these girls are never found

Never found never found

(Tracy Chapman, 3000 Miles, copyright 2001)

As a result of the Review story, Doug had several telephone calls including one from a resident of Montara, 14 miles north of the farm, claiming that she had actually seen Anna alive in 1976 in the company of a man called Bill.

She said Anna was brought to her house by a man who had some connection with her father and may have been a tenant. At the time of the incident the woman describes, she was sick in bed with an intestinal complaint. She didn't see a car.

Maureen and Mikie spoke to the woman on the telephone for an hour on Oct. 17, 2006). The woman believed very strongly that she saw Anna between September and November of 1976 at her home in Montara. She was quite passionate when she said "I know she's alive. I know she didn't drown." There were some inconsistencies in her story (such as saying that her present residence was where she saw Anna, and then saying that her father was building that house at the time) but the facts the woman furnished about herself and her background lined up with what we were able to learn by other means.

It is difficult to discount this informant's story, but also difficult to know where to take it. At the time she says she saw Anna, the informant was 17 years old, alone in the house, sick in bed, very close to having abdominal surgery, and she may have been on medication. She described a scene which took place 30 years previously; some parts were clear and some were not. The fact that she could not answer certain questions (such as whether Anna had lost baby teeth) and the fact that she was willing to speak with us for such a long time add, I think, to the possibility that we must take her story seriously, even if we do not know what to do with it.

She did not seem to be seeking attention, and the externals of her life seemed normal. She lives with her daughter and son. She doesn't use the computer, but her daughter has a wireless setup and the woman mentioned searching on "MySpace" for Anna. She did not know what WebSleuths was.

A few new impressions appeared. "Bill", the adult male who was in another room when "Anna" was speaking to the informant, called out "Michelle" and the informant thought that was the little girl's name. The presence of someone else in the house was not suggested previously. When the informant asked the little girl if that was her name, she said "no" and said (according to the informant) that her name was Anna Waters.

The informant said that the man, after telling her not to speak to the little girl, said something like "Michelle is her mother" and "she looks like her mother." I have sometimes answered to Michelle, but I don't think Anna would have called me that. When the informant talked to Doug, she said that the man said he had "taken" Anna, that he didn't want to "spend his life in a cage", etc.

The woman said that "Anna" cried at one point. She said that the little girl told her she was eight years old, but said that she looked older than eight. She again described her as having dark shoulder-length hair, not curly, and believes her eyes were brown, though she wasn't sure. She could not recall what the little girl was wearing, but said she seemed to be in good health.

Regarding the couple, the informant quoted the little girl as saying "They take care of me." That phrase set off a bell for me, since the real Anna would give things to people and say "Take care of this." Taking care of things was important to her, and she used this phrase frequently.

The informant doesn't believe the couple lived on the Coast or even in the coastal area. She had the impression that they lived in a house in San Mateo (a largish city on the other side of the coastal range), though she can't say why she thought this.

The woman said she had not seen any newspaper reports or television news about Anna's disappearance. It was the recent story in the Half Moon Bay Review which reminded her of this visit, and she never saw "Bill" again.

She seemed nervous. We did not tell the woman that I was Anna's mother. Anonymity seemed better; that way I could privately verify all the geographical details she offered without the possibility of her trying to sell me her story or feel overly emotional about doing so.

She said she remembered the child's name because at the time she related "Anna" to a friend of hers named "Anna Lee". She said the episode was strange to her, but that she managed to put it out of her mind until she read the recent newspaper story.)

An Answer to Our Prayers?

A woman named Robin H. contacted one of Anna's MySpace sites. She informed us that she had an acquaintance who strongly resembled the most recent age-progressed picture of Anna.

We have had numerous people contact us with pictures of people who look like what we believe Anna looks like today. In a world where an entire sub-genre of the entertainment industry exists to provide "look-alikes" of famous people, I have always used the standard of requiring "look-alike and something else" to get my attention. That something else could be a lot of things – the same name or birth date as Anna, being an adoptee, etc.

Robin's acquaintance had several "something else's". She was the youngest child in a large family, yet she felt that she did not belong. Her siblings teased her that she was adopted, though her mother claimed that she was not. She did not resemble her mother or her siblings. She had no memories of her life before age six and few before age ten. And, curiously, she was unable to locate a birth certificate on file for herself.

Robin, with the acquaintance's permission sent us a picture. The only request was that did not use her name on the forum. As a result, we gave her the alias "C". C's resemblance to the age progression of Anna was striking. Even certain imperfections such as moles and scarring from chicken pox matched up with Anna. A Websleuths member created a side-by-side comparison of Anna and C, even blending the two pictures to show how close of a resemblance existed:

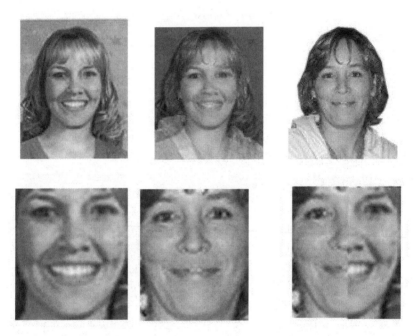

Anna is on the left. C is on the right.
The top center is a merge between the two.
The bottom right is a side-by-side composite.

Based on the strength of this resemblance, Mikie received a wonderful phone call: the San Mateo County Sheriff detective who had been assigned to Anna's case had been monitoring our progress and wanted to meet concerning this possible match for Anna.

Mikie and I met with three detectives concerning this latest development and provided the documentation for our finds. Based on the information, they eagerly agreed to conduct a DNA comparison between C and Anna.

DNA samples were collected from Mikie, Nonda and Ed. Also, Anna's bedroom slippers, which had not been washed since her disappearance, were collected in an attempt to cultivate a sample of Anna's DNA. Likewise, C submitted a sample to her local law enforcement, who were cooperating with San Mateo county. All of the various samples were sent to the crime labs of the California Attorney General's Office.

And the waiting started. Unlike such Hollywood images as C.S.I. where DNA results are instantaneously achieved by the push of a computer button by a provocatively dressed ex-underwear model, reality is much slower and certainly less sexy. Results usually take months, not minutes. "Cold cases" are assigned a lower priority than active cases where the results can either convict or clear suspects. And Anna's case was 34 years old – not high on the priority list. At least, not to the Attorney General's Office.

To the family and friends of Anna, the wait was interminable. We occupied the time by attempting to find anything that would link Anna to C – a family member who had lived in Half Moon Bay, a family friend whose name was familiar to both Mikie and C, anything.

As the months progressed, the fog that had clouded C's childhood memories began to clear. And as it did, amazing parallels began to emerge that convinced us more and more that we had found Anna.

C recalled an incident where she was riding a horse with some people other than her family. At first, Mikie did not see any connection. However, when reviewing her journal of their bus trip, Mikie discovered a mention of Anna riding a horse with family friends.

Some of C's recalled memories were hard to categorize – fleeting glimpses of a forgotten childhood that could not be matched up with Mikie's memories of Anna. People and events started to come back into C's cognition that no one – not even she – could explain.

C was asked if she recalled anything about a bus. Her immediate answer was no. Then she said, "Wait. It was a white bus with blue stripes." When questioned further about the shape of the bus, she said that it was flat on front, not like a hood on a car. This was an exact description of the color and shape of the bus that the family used during their trip – information that had never been published.

The most stunning recollection was of her laying on her back in a bed and reaching up above her head to rub something "fuzzy". When asked if she meant "fuzzy like a animal's fur?", she replied no, it was coarser than fur. When Mikie was informed of this memory, she thought she knew exactly what C meant. The three walls surrounding Anna's bed on the bus – including the wall directly behind her head, was covered with thick shag carpet. C had unwittingly described details of Anna's bed that had never been revealed before.

The string of amazing recollections only solidified what we had believed from the beginning – that C must be Anna. C herself was not convinced, but allowed for the possibility that she could be Anna. As the recollections mounted, so did our anticipation of the results.

Finally, we received word that the test was complete and had been mailed to the detective. We would find out the results the following week.

This set into play several simultaneous plans. One was to get all of the principals in place for a hoped-for reunion. C and Robin arranged for a plane flight to California if there was a match – paid for by the generosity of Robin's partner's company. I traveled to Half Moon Bay for the week with my wife so that I would be there for the results. And Mikie's brother Dan flew in from the East Coast.

Dan worked with CNN's New York bureau as a field cameraman and sound technician. Since he was the most familiar with the feeding frenzy that can accompany a story like this if it grabs the media's attention, he became the designated spokesman and media coordinator for the family.

A few months prior to this time, a young boy named Shawn Hornback that had been abducted several years earlier was discovered alive and well. The media circus that followed was a blueprint for exactly what we did not want to have if C was proven to be Anna.

Dan wisely recognized that the best way to control the media was to provide them with everything that they would need for a story…after everyone involved had come and gone. Dan evaluated the potential media sources and decided that the news show 48 Hours Mystery was the best suited to tell the story. Dan gave them exclusive access to Mikie and myself – along with footage that Dan would film of the results being revealed – with the understanding that nothing would be released until authorized by the family. They were to also immediately make certain film available to all media who requested it. This would eliminate the need for dozens of film crews camping out in front of Mikie's house for days hoping to get an "exclusive". The show agreed to Dan's requirements and a camera crew and producer were quickly dispatched.

While waiting for the results, the crew filmed some "back story". They filmed Mikie rehearsing with the Coastside Chorale for an upcoming concert. The first number on the program was "Sometimes I Feel Like a Motherless Child." Though it was obvious that "something was going on", the discretion showed by these professionals did not raise too much suspicion among the locals.

The crew also interviewed Mikie and myself for some background. During my interview, filmed in Mikie's backyard garden, the cameraman abruptly stopped filming. The producer asked why and the cameraman explained that the family cat, Mimi, had wandered into the background of the interview…and had proceeded to take a large on-camera dump. I told them that, somehow, I thought that a big-time network news interview would be a little more glamorous than having to deal with a cat's bowel movements. We all had a good laugh at the cat's expense.

Finally, we received the call that we had been hoping for – the detective had the results and was on his way to Mikie's house. I quickly called Robin so that she could be with her friend C when the results were read. Mikie and her husband Charles waited in the living room with Dan and his video camera. My wife and I joined the camera crew in the backyard as we gave the family the privacy that it deserved in this most trying moment. My mind raced with rerunning every step that we had taken that had brought us to this point. Mikie furiously played the piano, knowing that if she occupied her mind as we waited for the detective's arrival, she would not come unglued.

Finally, detective arrived. He spent several minutes with the family explaining the results. Those of us in the backyard held our breath, straining to hear anything that would reveal an answer. Charles eventually came to the back door. His eyes revealed the answer before his words ever could. There was no match.

We were stunned. I had hoped for the best and prepared for the worst, but slowly, secretly, hope had become optimism and optimism had become absolute belief that Anna had been found. But DNA does not lie.

The family took several minutes to digest the results and to compose themselves. Eventually, Mikie came to the backdoor and offered us coffee since we had been sitting in the Coastside fog for the better part of an hour.

The news crew, without camera or note-taking, came in and offered their sincere condolences to Mikie. The producer reminded Mikie that she had offered him a free piano lesson once this was all over. Mikie immediately said, "How about right now?" To everyone's delight and amusement, she had him playing a simple tune within minutes. The producer explained that the footage that had been shot would be inventoried to be used when we found Anna – not if, but when. These gentlemen were the antidote to the image of an uncaring and cruel press. They were a total class act.

(Experts back at the New York office also restored a degraded video of Anna and her family from 1971, made it into a DVD, and sent it to Mikie.)

The detective also called C and Robin with the results. I am sure that C felt both relief and a touch of sadness. C had shown great courage over the last few months – I cannot imagine what it would be like to suddenly face the possibility that everything that I had taken for granted about my life was a lie. She faced these questions without flinching. I am sure that the friendship and encouragement that Robin offered helped C during these months of uncertainty.

And the Band Plays On

After the results of the DNA test were posted on Websleuths, things slowed for a period. I know for myself, I was left drained of all energy for a time. I believe that many felt the same – the emotional rollercoaster left all of us wondering what the next step would be.

Once our energy was revived and our vigor returned, it became clear that the next step would be the same as all of the steps that had brought us so close to finding Anna. We had been doing everything right – we just needed to continue down the path until we find her.

The search for Anna is both a spiritual journey and spiritual warfare. We have learned as much about ourselves as we have about what happened to Anna. We have looked into the face of evil – an evil that can physically separate a mother and child, yet we have recognized that evil cannot spiritually separate a family.

My understanding of the mechanics of Christianity is that people are called to follow the Laws of the Old Testament - a calling that is impossible for fallen man to accomplish. However, once we have achieved everything humanly possible and still fall short of perfect Holiness, we call out for God and he makes up the difference so that we will recognize that only God can perform miracles.

I believe we face a similar struggle in the search for Anna. We must exhaust every human solution to this mystery, yet we may fall short. But just as we realize our own shortcomings, God may step in with another miracle to demonstrate that He is still in charge. Miracles still happen. They are God's way of showing us that He is still there and that He still cares. That He cares about things as large as the world and as small as one little missing girl.

So we search on.

CHAPTER TWENTY-ONE

No trace of Anna has been found, though we found many other things while looking. Maureen Wyenandt's searching for Anna has resulted in reuniting a half-dozen adoptees with their birth parents.

Maureen writes: "After being involved in Anna's case for several months I started looking through adoption message boards. I strongly felt Anna knew growing up that the people raising her were not her real family and she might now be looking for them. I started by posting on a few message boards looking for a female born in 1967 or 1968 and adopted in 1973."

On Monday, May 8, 2006, Maureen heard from an adoptee named Gloria, who said the family which raised her had told her she was adopted in 1973, a year after her birth mother died. Maureen found Gloria's birth record in California listed as Gloria S. and Gloria B. and searched death records to find a match with a woman having a maiden name of S. who died in 1972.

Maureen discovered that Gloria's birth mother had married two months before she died in a traffic accident. On Thursday Maureen contacted Gloria to let her know her mother's name and that of the man she had married. When Gloria discussed this with her mother-in-law, she learned that her birth mother had been expecting another child at the time of the accident. The baby survived a short period after the birth mother's death, and this helped confirm the identity through death records. By Saturday Maureen was able to locate in another state the man who had married Gloria's birth mother. He told Gloria where her mother was buried, a cemetery which was close to where Gloria grew up. The next day -- May 14, 2006 -- Gloria was able, after a separation of 34 years, to visit her mother's grave on Mothers Day.

"Over the next several months," Maureen writes, "I was reading every adoption site that I could find. I came across the FindMe mutual consent reunion registry. After making numerous inquiries about adoptees born in 1967, the volunteer sent me an e-mail asking who I was looking for. I spoke with the volunteer on the phone and explained Anna's story. The volunteer set me up on the Web site as a volunteer so that I could look for Anna myself."

In August, 2006, Maureen was looking for Susan, an adoptee born in Germany on September 25, 1967, Anna's birth day. Maureen was not able to locate Susan in Japan, where she was at the time she placed her information on the Web site, but since she listed her adoptive parents' names, Maureen was able to locate the adoptive mother. The mother gave Maureen Susan's Colorado phone number and Maureen was able to obtain more information on the birth parents. Susan was, indeed, born in Germany, but within days Maureen found her birth mother living in California. Her birth father is living in the U. S. and has not yet been located. Susan and her birth and adoptive mothers were reunited with each other.   .

"Many adoptees I've spoken with were eliminated as being Anna because they were adopted from birth and had many pictures of themselves from birth to the age of five," Maureen writes. After setting up a MySpace account for Anna, www.myspace.com/reuniteanna, Maureen received an e-mail from a woman whose friend thought the younger pictures of Anna were actually her own. Within two months DNA was submitted from the adoptee and compared to Anna's family, but after a four-month wait, the DNA comparisons showed that there was no match.

April was Maureen's next adoptee. Born in California and living in Washington, April's profile mentioned a man's name that is the same as mentioned in the book Searching For Anna, which Maureen had read in draft form. April also said she had two older brothers. It took Maureen five days to locate and make contact with April. After April told Maureen her birth mother's first name and date of birth, Maureen was able to locate her in Florida. Mother and daughter were reunited by telephone. April and her daughter plan to fly to Florida for a reunion with the birth mother and a sister in person.

Then came Jen. Jen was born on August 3, 1967 -- the day of Margaret Kukoda's death (George Brody once mentioned that Anna might be the reincarnation of Margaret). Jen remembered being told her name was Molly while in foster care before she was adopted at the age of 16 months. A birth record existed in San Francisco for Molly B. and Molly E. Maureen located Jen's birth mother. Jen wrote about her experience.

"Sometimes good things come out of bad things that happen, and in my case I was the one blessed by that scenario. I was adopted

40 years ago. I had always wanted to find and contact my birth parents, but I never wanted to hurt the parents that raised me my whole life, so I quietly intermittently searched without any success. Then after a tragic car accident both my adoptive parents were killed. It took several years for me to be able to start searching for my birth parents after that.

"One day I got the most amazing phone call from a woman -- telling me she was a "search angel" and she was contacting adoptees and trying to help them find their birth parents. She explained that she was doing this to help search for a missing woman named "Anna". Within a few weeks my life-long dream of knowing who my birth parents were came true. It was the most amazing experience, better that I had imagined my entire life. At first my birth mother didn't want to talk to me, but she finally did, and my life is so complete just by having that one phone conversation with her. I got to tell her that I have spent my whole life appreciating what she did for me, the totally loving sacrifice she made by giving me up for adoption. I told her she was amazing and strong and that I will always be grateful for her. It was truly a dream come true. I also was able to receive family medical history that could someday save my life or my children's lives.

"Although I was not the Anna that Maureen (my true angel) was looking for…I was reunited with my birth mother. I will always treasure that, and in turn I have put out the word in my circle of influence to raise awareness that we still need to find Anna and give her and her mother the wonderful gift I received.

"Thank you for letting me tell you my side of the Searching for Anna story."

Maureen has several other adoption cases awaiting more information. Trina, who was born in California in 1967, says that in 1972 or 1973 her adoptive family moved to England, where she now lives. She sent pictures of herself around the age of five which ruled her out as a match for Anna. Trina was told she was born in Los Angeles, but there were too many females born on the day in question to narrow down Trina's birth family. She has not yet received non-identifying information from the state.

Yet another adoptee born in California on Anna's birthday turned out to be a man named Kyle. Maureen located and forwarded his birth records, which other researchers had already sent. Maureen spoke with his birth mother and located his birth father in Hawaii. The parties have not yet made contact.

Another Susan, born in California in 1967, was adopted at birth, then relinquished back to the state around the age of three and adopted by another family at the age of five. Maureen made contact with the first adoptive family in California and they were able to answer questions for Susan. "They were quite surprised when they got my call," Maureen writes. "They were told by doctors that the adoptee would probably not live to be ten years old. They gave us her birth mother's last name as D. However, Susan has a birthmark that the adoptive mother denies she had. Questions still remain unanswered if Susan is the same child that the first adopted family gave back to the state."

A woman interested in Maureen's search told her of an adoptee, Sheri, who was searching for her birth parents. She believed she was born in California in January, 1967, and had been told a little about her birth mother by her adoptive father. Through an exhaustive search of marriage and birth records which included tracking down twins who would have been Sheri's half-siblings, Maureen located the birth mother, who did not want any contact with her child and refused to give any information about the birth father. She did agree to accept a letter from Sheri.

CHAPTER TWENTY-TWO

"We have visual memories from age five," Tink said in September, 2005. "Why hasn't she tried to get in touch with you?"

I think of everything we've done to try to find her. I think about the fact that I have moved twice since we lived on the farm where she disappeared; that Joe has moved several times, as have Nonda and Ed. I resumed my maiden name, and I doubt that she ever knew it. Nonda, who knew only Greek, no English, at the age of five, now remembers only a few words of Greek. Transplanting a child at the age of five can eliminate a native language. And who knows, if she was abducted, what Anna might have been told about her origins and her family. Certainly not the truth.

I have vivid memories from the age of five (though at this point I may not remember the plot of a film I saw last week.) I remember the day that scratches on a page congealed into words and I could read. I remember being stumped by the word "wagon" in a kindergarten book. I remember my kindergarten teacher, Miss Ella, who wore laddered stockings (this was 1941, and it was hard to get good stockings.) I remember having whooping cough and not being able to get my breath. I remember waking in the night, thinking I had not had dinner, and crying until my mother came into the room and reminded me what we had had for dinner. But I only know the town we lived in because the family has mentioned it over the years. I don't think I ever knew what street we lived on, or our telephone number, if we had a telephone.

For many years, I would drive out to Purisima Canyon and park and sit and think about Anna, going over what I knew and did not know, wondering if I would ever solve the mystery of her disappearance.

In music, even music which has been played by thousands of people for hundreds of years, sometimes a new thing will come out of old material: The performer stumbles across a melodic fragment, then finds it connected to an inner voice in the other hand, and suddenly a theme which had hidden within the chords will emerge, its existence previously unsuspected. It seemed possible that some new understanding might come from the facts of Anna's disappearance.

In the beginning, my faith that Anna was all right, wherever she was, was unflagging. Though sometimes I felt that I, not Anna, was missing, I was sure that whatever happened to her had happened for a reason, that there would prove to be some meaning which was not yet apparent. I was so weightless that I hardly needed sleep or food. I could read nothing but scripture, anybody's scripture; other writing seemed as heavy as boulders.

Little by little, I became heavier--or denser. Only I, it seemed, could live with not knowing. Whenever the subject came up, no one could resist suggesting some course of action, even though after the first year we had tried almost everything. After a while, the implied course of action was that I should try to stop thinking about it.

I could not stop thinking about it. I combed through all the possibilities, mad, sordid, impossible as some of them seemed. I examined closely the possibility that I did not want to know what became of her, that I couldn't stand knowing. As Joe was willing to take apart the creek with his hands, so I was willing, I concluded, to know, no matter how terrible the knowing was.

In 1985 or 1986, Joe left home and eventually we were divorced. My old friend Howard Gilligan died and I moved into his house. I went to Greece for my sixtieth birthday. I was living alone, with one son in Seattle and one in Los Angeles. My sister Jo and my mother went with me, and the two of us sat in an outdoor restaurant in Philothei, where I had once lived, and talked with Tony Trimis about the children each of us had lost. Mother's son and my brother Lindle had died of leukemia at the age of five. Tony and Elli's young daughter Marina had been killed in a car accident. Jo's son Lindle Morris, a robust young man, had been found dead while fishing at their Tennessee home.

Years later, Jo wrote me: " I had forgotten the conversation until you mentioned it... there was the conversation in the recesses of my mind which almost always is the same: I wonder how it feels to have no experience of sharing growing-up years for Mother's Lindle; how can Mikie bear not knowing, but at least she has the possibility of hope; thankfulness that Lindle was with me on his last day... and always there is that warning, "tread lightly, tread lightly, and don't get too deep because others might feel just as you do that to do so would produce such a torrent of tears, it might not be possible to cut them off." And of course it's okay, yes, it's such a nice thing for me that anyone wants to talk about Lindle; most of the time it's as if he never lived."

The teenaged brother of a piano student lost control of his bicycle, was hit by a car and died. The mother called me from the hospital to cancel the student's lesson. Her voice, barely audible, was anguished. The worst part, she said, is the unanswered questions. Was he in pain? Was he afraid? Half Moon Bay High School erected a small memorial for the boy, a Star of David, outside the band room.

I watched a documentary film, "My Cyprus", by Barnabas Zagaris. A Greek-American father whose 17-year-old son had been taken by Turkish Cypriot soldiers in Cyprus and never heard from again held a photograph of the boy, a dark-eyed youth wearing a cross. "Just let my boy go," the father said to the camera, his face impassive. "I forgive you. I will not blame you or seek revenge or sue you. Just set my boy free."

I felt that I knew that father, knew that thought. But after so many years, if Anna were alive and remembered, would she not try to find her way home?

Twenty years after her disappearance, I donated some of her toys to a local group which was collecting toys for poor children at Christmas. I kept her record player, her records, and her rock collection, a huge stuffed frog Gloria Barron made for her, a teddy bear from her paternal grandparents. The big redwood cradle was taken apart and put in a box.

As I calculated what her age and size would be, I took some of her small dresses and made them into quilt pieces. A quilted Star of Bethlehem from Anna's old clothes became a skirt for the Christmas tree, and my mother framed one quilt square and put it in her bedroom. The daisy costume, the leopard-print bathrobe, her cowboy boots were packed away but taken out for cleaning from time to time. A friend took one of Anna's paintings of a smiling flower and put it in a stained glass frame.

The Websleuths forum asked all the questions once again, and although answering them was difficult at first, it became reassuring as we once again examined all known aspects of Anna's story. My brother Dan, after first looking at the WebSleuths forum, said "I had no idea. They're like the Baker Street irregulars" (referring to Sherlock Holmes' assistants in the Arthur Conan Doyle books.)

Soon the search expanded to an extent which would have been unimaginable in 1973. On a given day in November, 2007, Anna's case in WebSleuth's Spotlight Cases had 38 threads or topics with

6,696 posts which had had 283,422 views. Doug's "Holy cow!" and "Holy Toledo!" frequently appeared on the forum as some new avenue was opened.

All expertise and fees for various services were contributed. Apart from a replacement computer donated to one of the sleuths by another member, no goods or money changed hands.

Forum members ranged as far south as Australia, as far north as Canada, and as far East as England. Through the YouTube Missing Children's Channel's International Centre for Missing and Exploited Children, a WebSleuths member sent a video of Anna which circulates worldwide. A WebSleuths member even identified my kindergarten teacher of 65 years previous, Miss Ella Wortham, in Leitchfield, Kentucky, and sent me Miss Ella's obituary, which said she had been a woman noted for her frugality and self-reliance.

After the Review article appeared, Doug was contacted by the woman who had driven the school bus the day Anna disappeared. The driver, however, could not recall seeing anything unusual on Jan. 16, 1973.

The forum found Kelly, Anna's friend at Hatch School, who wrote:
"I was a friend and classmate of Anna's and we shared the same birth date and were both born in San Francisco. I can remember the day our teacher told us that Anna had 'disappeared.'… The only one (in the class) I remember is Anna, her curly hair, her smile and her laughter. She was fun. I have learned more about her disappearance through this forum than I ever knew. My mother was the afternoon kindergarten teacher and Anna and I went to the morning kindergarten with Mrs. R. Both my mom and Mrs. R. have ALWAYS believed that Anna was abducted."

The classmate, Kelly, recalled Anna's cowboy boots. "I remember Anna. I remember."

Steve Loftin, a forensic artist at the National Center for Missing and Exploited Children, had produced two heart-stopping portraits of Anna, one as she might have looked at the age of 40, and another at an estimated age of 17 or 18, to be compared to viewers' high school yearbooks. The NCMEC unit responsible for age-advanced pictures has located some 800 missing children since its creation 17 years ago.

One of these cases involved Steve's age-advancement from a photograph of a 47-day-old infant who had been missing for 21 years. The young man, who has since survived a tour in Afghanistan and Iraq, was identified by a colleague after seeing the composite Steve created.

Gerald Nance at the National Center for Missing and Exploited Children wrote:

"Anna's case is far from (our) oldest. I have two cases from the 1940s, a few from the 50s, and a good bunch from the 60s. I know that after this much time, your question becomes 'Is she alive?'

"We have several factors in our corner to suggest that she is: Most children taken under the age of five (and the percentage gets higher as the age gets lower) are taken because the abductor wants or needs a child for family reasons. The issues of sexual assault are usually found in older kids, (age) ten and up.

"It is possible for (Anna) not to have any memory of family. It is never a factor of time to say that after so many years, etc.

"You also need to be able to stand in today's world and (give) energy to your family and friends. You have been through so much and there is much more to do. Your energies elsewhere do not suggest that you forget or cover up. It is a release that enables you to function today…"

A WebSleuths member wrote: "I have learned that tragedy need not define us."

These pages tell everything I know about the search for Anna. I have presented the facts as truthfully as possible, given what I know and do not know. The Appendices have maps for reference and tell about various people who figure in Anna's story. Forum updates, background information, and links to various articles and videos are now found on www.searchingforanna.com.

I have not spent all of the past 35 years searching for Anna, though sometimes it seems that way. In 1974, a year after Anna disappeared, we did The Fantasticks in Half Moon Bay, so that when Skyline College was auditioning for the show a few years later, I took my score and tried out. I played the show, then I became a staff accompanist, and then I became part of the teaching staff in the music department. I taught several thousand students over a period of 18 years before retiring in May, 2005.

Joe Ford continued his journey on his own in 1985, but has stayed in touch with the family and contributed to the Websleuths investigation.

My sons Nonda and Ed are grown and marvelously successful in their work. I have five accomplished grandchildren.

In 1998, Charles Calvert and I were married. My friend K. recently reminded me of the three-word speech I gave at the time (I was 62 years old): "Never give up." We have been to Greece several times; the two of us play in the community orchestra. We live quietly in Montara in a house which in the early part of the Twentieth Century was called the Von Suppé Poet and Peasant Cottage of the Montara Fine Arts Country Club. The house was given to me by Howard Gilligan, who painted the portrait of Anna used in this manuscript. We attend Holy Trinity Greek Orthodox Church in San Francisco. The priest prays for Anna.

I tried writing this book in 1996. But even 23 years after Anna's disappearance, I had trouble making myself examine the scarier aspects of the case. Now, after 35 years, I find that finally I can write about what happened without feeling I have two-ton weights attached to me. Doug French's interest in reopening the investigation had everything to do with my completing and updating the manuscript. And memory is so strange that writing one scene would conjure up ten others, things I probably repressed before.

If it seems odd that the melodrama, "The Saga of Spanishtown Sue", dealing with a stolen daughter, was produced three months before Anna disappeared, consider this: In 1963, four years before Anna was born, I wrote a bad and fortunately unpublished novel in which a character thinks her daughter has gone into the ocean and tries to follow her, calling out her name--Anna.

Sometimes we seem to dream our children before we have them. Loss of the child in these cases is a double loss--of the dream as well as of the person. How many ways can you lose a child? By the failure to conceive, by miscarriage, abortion or stillbirth, by disease, crime, war or simple alienation; by divorce, age, abandonment, by the failure of the reality to mesh with the dream.

My neighbor Mary DeLong in her book "Grace Notes" has an exquisite poem entitled "Passage":

Like a gift long anticipated,
His nature had been revealed,
With the shuffling of the cards,
Yet details left still to envision.
Preparing the dream.
Pulled by forces unknown,
Our poet boy was called away.
Suddenly lost, lost.
Leaving behind only shadows of expectation.

One Mother's Day, I accompanied the Skyline College vocal jazz ensemble in a small concert for women in the San Bruno prison. "Many of them have children," a guard explained to us, "and this is a particularly hard day for them to be away from their families." We did spirituals, sweet old songs, upbeat jazz pieces. The prisoners, doleful and suspicious when first all these straight people came into the room, began to sing along. I imagined that the loss of their children by separation was as difficult as if someone had stolen the children away.

With all these perils, it is no wonder that we received so many warnings as children: Don't put your arm out the car window. Don't pet strange dogs. Don't sit on the toilet seat. Never take anything from a stranger. Don't speak to people you don't know. It makes me think of Bob Dylan's song, "Masters of War": "You've thrown the worst fear that can ever be hurled/ The fear to bring children into the world..." Yet there is a limit to how much we can protect a child; we don't want to make him or her fearful and crazy.

The letter from Usch (Thulten Chosang), our friend who wrote from Dharmsala about the human need to know, is pertinent. In 1974, I went back to school and learned some things which helped me search: All sound proceeds from silence (Charles Gustavson).   Things are not always as they appear; Mercury does not move backward in the sky (Michael Chriss).

Weight is our enemy, my piano teacher Robert Sheldon said, speaking specifically about piano technique, but also of attitude.   In summer of 1996, rather hoping from some inspiration from the Oracle at Delphi, I instead received it from my mother, Fran Benedict, who said "Everyone is responsible for his own understanding."

Just as Anna's little garden with its creek mint and forget-me-not became dispersed into the larger landscape, the mystery of her disappearance and my attempts to resolve it have dispersed over time into a larger mystery.

In one sense, surely our missing children are lost to us, but in another sense they are found: We hold them within ourselves and our love for them is returned to us. We look upon the world with different eyes because of them. Perhaps they also have made us more aware of the fragility and value of human life, or made us more understanding of loss and those who have survived it.

If you have ever lost someone and could not reason why, you are not alone. By enduring what you may believe you cannot endure, and by doing so with as good a face as you can manage, you will receive compensations. Silence prepares the way for sound.   The skyscape changes from hour to hour. Whether you live in the loss of the one you loved or celebrate the life you had for a time is ultimately a matter of choice. We are each responsible for our own understanding.   These lost children live in our hearts and minds, forever young, never changing; they are always with us.

APPENDIX A

DRAMATIS PERSONAE
and their whereabouts as of January, 2008

ANNA CHRISTIAN WATERS: Born Sept. 25, 1967 in San Francisco. Disappeared from Half Moon Bay Jan. 16, 1973. Whereabouts unknown.

The Pimentel Ranch on Purisima Creek Road. Now called Rancho Canada Verde after the Spanish land grant name, Canada de Verde y Arroyo de la Purisima. Owned by Tracy Chapman, the pop singer. In 1973, the farm was the last group of structures on the road, but there are now houses extending to the former Hatch Woods, now Purisima Creek Redwoods Open Space Preserve.

Parents: Mother, Michaele Benedict, Montara, California, music teacher. Father, George, M.D., married to Benedict March 25, 1965, died January, 1982.

Brothers: Epaminondas (Nonda) Antonios Trimis, born 1958, lives in Seattle. Musician and architect.

Edward Antonios Trimis, musician and educator, born 1961, married to Moira Thomas May 28, 1983, lives in La Crescenta, California.

Other Trimises: Dr. Antonios Epaminondas Trimis, father of Nonda and Ed, married to Michaele Benedict Jan. 1, 1956, divorced in 1964; Married to Elli since 1965. Children: Antigone, born June 4, 1966, Marina, who died July 1, 1981, and Alexander, born Aug. 18, 1983.

Stepfather: Joseph Edward Ford, married to Benedict September 16, 1972 and for 15 years after that.

Detective Brendan Maguire, later Sheriff of San Mateo County. Died unexpectedly during reelection campaign in 1986, but still won 79 per cent of the vote. San Mateo County Correctional Facility bears his name.

Maternal grandparents: Fran Benedict, genealogist, born May 16, 1918, now living in Cookeville (Putnam County), Tennessee. Grandfather, Edward Lindle Benedict, died October 30, 1984.

Uncles and Aunt: Les Benedict, musician, living in Los Angeles. Dan Benedict (AnnasUnc and webmaster of www.searchingforanna.com), living in New Jersey. Jo Walker, living in Clinton, Tennessee

Great-grandmother: Mamie Demaris Chambers Ensor (Nannie), died Aug. 18, 1975.

Paternal grandparents: Anna Waters., retired nurse and medical missionary, living in Wisconsin. Dr. Henry Waters. died October 11, 1975.

Teacher: Ruth Rafello, who with Janice Brown taught Anna's kindergarten class at Hatch School in Half Moon Bay in 1973; retired master teacher, lives in Montara.

Purisima Neighbors: Peggy and John, living in California. Their now-grown daughters Gina, Shawn, and Daisy. Suzanne, now living in North Carolina. Bill --lives in Russian River, California. Godparents: Phil, married to Jill, still living and practicing medicine in San Francisco. Former wife Elizabeth now living in Oregon. Their grown children Joshua, an environmentalist, and Rachael (Alex), a researcher in plant genetics.

Other friends: Dr. George Stewart and Dr. Poki Namkung, who when last contacted were living in the east Bay with their children N. (Joseph's godson) and A.

Arlene, nurse and writer, living in San Francisco. Her son Baris-John , living in San Francisco. Asya, John's father, club owner in Cyprus.

Dr. Dick, living in San Francisco with his beautiful wife K.

Byron, living in San Rafael.

Members of Farmers' Feed, the food club: Bryant, Gene, Pabby, Byron of the Palace Ranch, the Freemans, Stan, Linda. (Bryant and Pabby still live on the Coastside; Linda lives in Hawaii.)

Josiah Thompson (Tink): philosopher, author and private investigator, worked on Anna's case in 1978, again in 1980, and again in the fall of 2005.

Lindsay Mickles: Owner of the farm on Purisima Creek Road. Mickles Enterprises, Petaluma, California.

George Brody or Brodie (also called "Bobby"): Mentor of George Waters, died December, 1981, of throat cancer.

APPENDIX B: MAPS

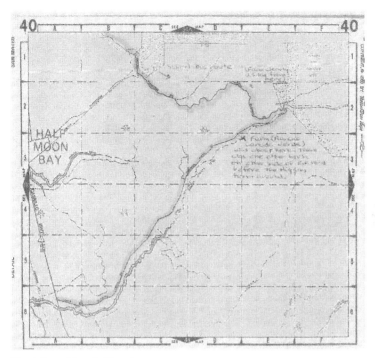

Purisima Creek Road

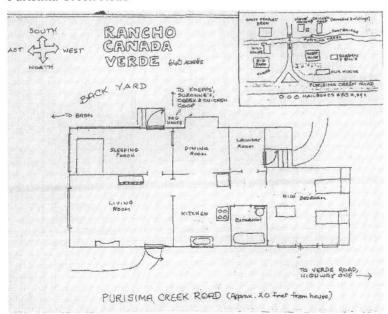

Diagram of the House

APPENDIX C: ANNA"S DRAWINGS

Mom (Michaele)

Joka (Joe Ford)

Anna's Self Portrait

Friends

THANK YOU

Thousands of people have been involved in the search for Anna, some of them known to us only by their screen names on the WebSleuths forum. Doug and I are deeply grateful to all these generous and kindly individuals. In particular, we would like to thank the following:

Jerry Nance, Anna's case director at the National Center for Missing and Exploited Children, and Steve Loftin, the Center's gifted forensic artist.

Detective Jim Gilletti at the San Mateo Sheriff's Department.

Tricia Griffith, owner of WebSleuths.

Maureen Wyenandt

Dan Benedict, creator of www.searchingforanna.com

Robin Hardy

Marc Longpre at the Half Moon Bay Review

Peggy Walla, handwriting expert and private detective

Gina Moyer, videographer

Peter Henderson, CBS News producer

A special thank-you to the spouses, Debi French, Terry Wyenandt, Charles Calvert and Anne Levin Benedict for their understanding and indulgence.

ABOUT THE AUTHORS

Michaele Benedict is a mother, a musician and a poet. She is a retired teacher and a former newspaper woman. She currently resides in coastal Northern California.

Douglas French spends his days working in the printing industry and his nights entertaining as a singer. He currently lives in the foothills of Northern California.

Made in the USA
Middletown, DE
08 November 2020